This is my Book

FROM

"THAT'S ALL RIGHT," TIM REPLIED. "SIT DOWN WHILE YOU'RE
WAITING."

"The Door in the Mountain."   (See page 17)

THE DOOR
IN THE
MOUNTAIN

A MYSTERY STORY FOR GIRLS

BY

IZOLA L. FORRESTER

ILLUSTRATED

CUPPLES & LEON COMPANY
PUBLISHERS   NEW YORK

THE DOOR
IN THE
MOUNTAIN

The Door
in the
Mountain

CHAPTER I

It was Saturday morning and no one had
thought to call Timmie. When she awakened she
lay drowsily watching the ceiling overhead where
the ivory colored plaster had cracked until it
looked like an old map. Then she whistled, a
long, clear piercing whistle warranted to reach to
the far limits of the McLean household and
signal the boys she was wide awake. It died
away on the still, fragrant air and to Timmie's
surprise and suspicious indignation, there came
no answering hail, nothing at all. Outside it was
hot and a golden haze seemed to hang over the
mesa and canyon, but there was no sound.

Timmie listened intently and sprang out of
bed. Very well, she thought as she dressed in a
hurry, if they didn't want to answer her, she supposed they had had breakfast without her and

gone down to the corral to play with Pablo and the ponies. " Jippers," she called them scornfully in her mind. This came of being the only girl with a whole raft of brothers. Life was just one fight after another for self-preservation. But when they needed her, they could be so sweet and interested in everything she was doing. Just wait, that's all.

She sauntered out on the long narrow veranda that ran the whole length of the one-story house, scanning the landscape out of the corner of her eye for hidden enemies. But there was no one in sight until she turned the corner stealthily and almost tumbled over the stretched out figure of Pablo sound asleep with his head on a sack of chicken feed. Anyway, she knew now the boys were not with him. She walked around him disdainfully. Another boy. The world was crammed with them, all doing just as they pleased when you wanted them to do something different. And now she made another disturbing discovery as she came to the screened door of the dining-room. She was very hungry and there wasn't a sign of any breakfast ready for her when she went inside.

It was such a cool, shaded little room something like the refectory down at St. Michaela's
school where Estrella's youngest children went.
Plain stucco walls with high deeply set windows,
very wide and on each embrasured sill a squat
Mexican jar overflowing with yellow poppies
and brilliant blue lupines. There was the long
narrow table with chairs of dark oak to match.
Over in the corner hung a bunch of dried gourds,
orange and a mottled green and coral one, mixed
with drying red peppers that Estrella was liable
to festoon in any handy place.

It was all very cool and pleasant, but the table
was bare and the kitchen beyond was empty.
Feeling more and more abused Timmie took a
look at the clock. Twenty minutes after eight,
early enough for Saturday when one had to rise at
six every other week-day, practise for a whole hour
on the piano before breakfast; then half an hour
to eat breakfast and dash to school. Sometimes
you didn't dash if the old car failed to start. And
here was a beautiful day all free and clear, and
just because she had overslept everybody had
gone and left her. All right, she thought
haughtily, let them; and by them she meant

Don and Neil. Who really cared? Everything went wrong when Mother was away. She hunted around until she found oranges, milk, a loaf of fresh bread and two eggs. When Estrella came in from the garden she found a very distant young person at the kitchen table absorbed in eating breakfast and reading a book.

"Hot," said Estrella happily, as she dumped a mass of freshly gathered vegetables from her ample apron on to the floor, and knelt to sort them out. "Too much hot."

Tim regarded her with a calm and restrained expression. This was one of Tim's specialties. Her large gray blue eyes would become very distant and even contemptuous in their careless gaze, then her long black lashes which curved up anyway on their own account, seemed to become even more "topliftical," and, as Neil said disgustedly, Timmie would look at one as if one were a ruined ham.

"Where are the boys?" asked Tim.

"Eat much, much breakfast." Estrella sorted beans carefully, red from white. "Go hunt rabbit."

"They did, did they?" Tim exploded. "Of

all the cold-blooded, fiendish things to do when they knew I wanted to go to Sandy's to-day. Why didn't you call me, Estrella, when you saw what they were doing?"

Estrella shrugged her shoulders and smiled the odd little one-sided smile she had. "Pablo tell me he see the dogs run after them. I no can call—all gone."

"Then why didn't Pablo yell to them to wait for me?" said Tim despondently. "Only he wouldn't, he's another one. Now I've got to stay around here all day long Saturday, and nothing to do but watch you cook and cook and Pablo sleep his head off like a lizard."

"You go ride," suggested Estrella mildly. "Nice long ride?"

"And bake myself out there in the desert? No, thanks. I wanted to go when it was early and cool." Tim got up and went out on the back stoop. The pepper trees around the house trailed their long fern-like branches to the terra cotta tiled roof. A couple of mocking birds hopped inquisitively around the yard eyeing Timmie and expecting their usual breakfast from her, but she looked past them to the long view of the canyon

as it swept down toward Frisbee. She was
thinking it might be fun to take Chapo and ride
into town and buy something if it was only an
ice cream cone, anything enticing to dangle so to
speak before the boys later on.

The McLean ranch occupied a low mesa that
seemed to extend like a shelf from the rocky side
of Las Flores Canyon. The ranch house itself
looked quite small and insignificant if you happened to catch sight of it from the mountain stage
road, just a low stucco rambling house with the
red tiled roof half hidden among the pepper trees.
But when you came indoors you found its large
low ceilinged rooms stretching out on all sides.
Mr. McLean said he had bought the old original
house from a Mexican, and had added all the
unexpected little wings as afterthoughts when
the children were born. It made it very con-
venient because each had their own room now,
wide apart from the others.

The outbuildings started from Estrella's
kitchen and rambled down hill to the corral and
barns. And this was another odd thing about the
ranches around Frisbee, Tim had noticed, just
as soon as an easterner bought one he built a real

barn. She started down for the corral now to find out how many ponies were gone. Dusty and Quien Sabe were missing, which meant Don and Neil had absconded with them and the dogs too, but her own Chapo dozed in the shade with Buckskin, Tom's horse. Maybe it would be better, she thought, to take Estrella's suggestion, and ride out after the boys and surprise them after they thought they'd lost her for a whole day. Only she didn't feel like chasing rabbits, hunting scurrying bunnies all over the dry sandy sagebrush around Sandy's place. She only liked to visit Sandy when he could sit and tell stories and he'd never have a chance if the boys were around.

She climbed to the top rail of the corral and perched there, her chin on her hands, looking off at the rose and ochre mountains that banked the skyline beyond the canyon. Where the earth had crashed in after heavy rains the jagged rock lay exposed in vari-colored layers, making narrow ledges where lizards sunned themselves and a few flowers managed to grow. Here and there down the barren slopes there grew stunted trees half toppling over that were very handy to hold to

when one was clambering down to the bottom of
the canyon. This was one of Tim's favorite
places when the creek had water in it, but now
it was dry, so there was no fun in going down
there, she thought.

Along the side of the creek bed ran the winding old wagon road that had led to Frisbee before
the new motor highway had gone through to Oro
where the smelters were, thirty-five miles away.
Tim had been down to Oro but she liked her own
little half-dead town better. Mr. McLean was
consulting engineer down at one of the mining
companies in Oro, and Tom, Jr., went to High
School there, so they always left the ranch around
six-thirty and took the wagon road because it was
a short cut.

Frisbee had long since outlived its own boom,
but there had been a gold rush there once. Sandy
had come out in it, he told her, when the wagon
road for miles away was lined with wagons and
teams, anything that would travel. Tents and
shacks sprang up everywhere overnight and Main
Street had seemed just like a circus with flags
flying and peanut and popcorn stands and all
kinds of little shows. Then in a few months the

mines had petered out and the people had drifted on to the next gold stampede.

Sandy had known people, he said, who had followed gold rushes for years and years all the way from Alaska down to Mexico. He said he never felt like keeping after them himself. He liked to stay put where he had the mountains and desert and plenty of rest time. Besides, Frisbee was picturesque where Oro was plain ugly with nothing at all but the smelters and shacks and a few stores. In Frisbee you had two churches and the mission and the big Central School that stood on a whole block of its own with a gymnasium and playground and auditorium. Tim agreed with Sandy that only people who could afford to stay where they wanted to could appreciate Frisbee. Tourists and business folks just rushed by it as fast as they could. Which was just as well, Tim thought, because who wanted them anyway?

She swung down from the rail and went over to the shed that served as a garage for the two cars, her father's roadster and the old runabout that the boys had named Leaping Lena. It certainly seemed almost human sometimes. Once

when they had been late to school it had stopped
dead half-way to town, and the boys had
worked and worked to start it up again, and it
just wouldn't go. So Timmie in despair had
stood in front of it shaking her fist at it, and
saying:

"You know perfectly well what you're doing
to us, Lena, you're going to make us late, and
we'll get into trouble and have to stay after
school, and I think you're just as mean as you
can be after all we've done for you. You
wouldn't even be running at all if we didn't make
you." Then the boys tried to start it up again
and the engine went, for no reason at all; so Timmie always said Lena understood her.

She ran the car out of the shed and decided
with the boys away she'd clean it up in her own
way which meant principally in heaving endless
buckets of water at it from the drinking trough.
She was carrying about the nineteenth when Estrella called to her excitedly from the kitchen
door, making wild motions behind her. Tim
thought, "Now, what?" but she set the pail
down and was half-way to the house before she
saw there were callers. A large closed car stood

in the roadway outside the wire fence, and a chauffeur waited at the front door.

Two things occurred instantly to Tim and she started on a run for the house. There wasn't any bell for him to ring, and if he tried to ask Estrella anything, she'd never understand him. When you talked to Estrella you had to use both sign language and pigeon-toed English, Neil said. So Tim made short work of the distance and went to the front door herself.

CHAPTER II

" How do you do? " she said, opening it unexpectedly. " There isn't any bell."

" Oh, yes, quite so," the chauffeur smiled at her cheerfully. " Curious, I was looking everywhere for one. I wonder if you'd be so kind as to direct us back to the highway. We seem to have lost it, somehow, a few miles back."

" Fifteen miles back. Did you come across the desert from those mountains over there? " Tim pointed at her pet range, the Horseshoe.

" Possibly, I couldn't say, we just kept travelling. We're bound for a place called Frisbee —— "

" It's right down the canyon two miles." Tim was keeping one eye on the strange car. A girl and a boy were getting out, both about her own age, and someone was telling them to stay in the car, a stout woman with fuzzy fair hair and a veiled hat. The veil was thrown back and she seemed hot and distracted, but neither the girl nor the boy took any notice of her. They came toward the house together.

" Will you see if we may get a drink of water, Chester? " asked the girl, not looking at Tim.

" If I might, Miss," Chester smoothed over the curtness of the request. " Sorry to make you any trouble." .

" That's all right," Tim replied. " Sit down while you're waiting if you'd like to." She went back to the kitchen and told Estrella to fill the big orange earthenware pitcher with cool water from the well, and carried it out herself with Estrella behind her carrying glasses. Both the girl and boy stared curiously at the dark skinned smiling Mexican woman with her sparkling friendly brown eyes and gleaming white teeth. Tim was like a straight backed slim young boy in her riding trousers and shirt, her Saturday dress, ready for emergencies. She returned their stare with cool interest until they looked away from her.

The chauffeur had gone back to the car and was trying to explain the right direction, but evidently making no progress. Suddenly the girl called down a streak of French that startled

Tim and seemed to satisfy the other person in the car perfectly. She nodded her head over and over and waved her hand at them, calling, " Bien, bien, merci."

" Tumpy can't speak English at all. She's our governess. Is there a hotel at Frisbee, do you know? "

" We're not going to a hotel, Margot," protested the boy. " Father said it was a private house, Mrs. Barney's."

" Turn when you get to the square with the Soldiers' Monument, and it's the third house on Sierra Bonita Avenue. There are only three houses on that street so you can't miss it. It's the one with the windmill. Mrs. Barney came out in the gold rush and she tried to start a real hotel here, but there wasn't anyone to stop there afterwards, so she just stayed on herself. But it's the only place where you get running water, and she has a splendid cook. Over at the National Hotel the cook's a Chinaman, but he left yesterday."

" I see, thank you." The girl hesitated and looked at the boy. Tim knew just exactly how they understood each other without having to say anything. She was that same way with Don. "Our name is Thorpe, I'm Margot and this is my brother Dick."

"I'm Katherine Campbell McLean," said Tim cordially. "If you like, I'll show you the way out of the canyon and make sure you hit the highway again. Wait a minute." She set down the water pitcher and ran down to the corral, threw a saddle on Chapo, and was wheeling back on the pony in no time. Estrella stood on the veranda, watching the start of the big car following after the dancing feet of Chapo along the wagon road until they were out of sight. Then she sighed with relief. At least Tim had found some excitement to keep her busy.

The boys would certainly have said Tim was showing off, either herself or Chapo. Knowing she had an attentive audience right behind her, she could not resist letting the pony do all its usual stunts, rear and buck a little, and sidestep gaily. And when they came out on the motor highway she decided to keep on going into town, not as guide any longer, but galloping ahead as far as the post office with the hope of finding a letter from her mother. Of course she kept an

eye on the car over one shoulder to make sure it
turned at the Monument and went down to Mrs.
Barney's.

The post office was in Sam's store. The iron
hitching rail outside of Sam's always had several
horses standing but not hitched. Tim slid down
from the saddle and left Chapo exchanging
greetings with several neighbors.

"Hello, Timmie, how's the world?" called
Sam heartily as he saw her from behind the vin-
egar barrel.

"Fine. Got a letter for me?"

"Sure." Sam came out wiping his hands on
his apron and dove behind the little wooden
boxed-in space where it said "Post Office." He
shuffled a package of letters over from a dusty
pigeonhole, and handed out one postmarked
"Buffalo."

"Right one, eh? When's your ma coming
back?"

"Pretty soon." Tim read the letter with absorbed delight, disregarding Sam's interest in its
contents entirely.

"Is she feeling fit, all the folks well?" he
asked mildly.

" All except Dinah. She died." Tim's face was sober as a judge over Sam's deep concern. " She was the old black cat. And Mother won't be home for another month." She stuffed the letter in her trousers pocket and scowled, her eyes fixed on the open doorway.

" See that big car go by just now?" asked Sam to divert her. " That belongs to the New York consulting engineer of the Hayes-Roberts interests. That's the most important thing that's happened in the town of Frisbee in fourteen years."

" No, it isn't. I'm only thirteen, Sam." Tim perched on a couple of empty boxes handy to an open box of saltines and a keg of ripe olives. " I'll bet a cookie I can tell you more about him than you can. He's got two children and their names are Dick and Margot, and there's a French governess that can't speak English, and the chauffeur's named Chester."

" Well, is that so, Tim?" Sam pushed another box over to her. " Try some of these dates, just got 'em in. Where they going to stop, do you know? "

" Certainly I know," said Tim carelessly.

"Over at Mrs. Barney's. They lost their way and came along the wagon road by the ranch and I found out all about them."

"Gee, you are the luckiest kid I ever saw, never miss anything. Hear how long they were staying at Frisbee?"

"No, but they've got lots of baggage strapped all around the car inside and out. And Sam," she was confidential now that the news was out, "the boys weren't home at all. They got up and left me flat this morning and went hunting rabbits over at Sandy's. Wait till they find out what they missed."

"Well, since you let me in on the news," said Sam, "I'm going to tell you something else surprising. Looka' here."

He tiptoed to the back of the store with Tim following, and drew aside the brightly flowered strip of cretonne that served as curtain between the store and his own private quarters. Tim looked in at the back room where Sam cooked and slept. Someone was sound asleep on the couch in a corner, covered over with a gray blanket.

"Who is it?" she asked eagerly. Sam beckoned her back into the store.

" Came through on the stage this morning early, all the way from Austin, Texas. Yes, ma'am, and he said he hadn't slept a wink on the road, he was so afraid the stage was going to topple over. It does take nerves and good experience to sleep on them things. I knew what he'd been through, and I told him to bunk in there, and sleep all he wanted to. He's from the same state I am."

" I never knew you came from Texas, Sam."

" Didn't," retorted Sam proudly. " Came out here from Indiana. He's a professor of geology —no, wait a minute, I've got him wrong. It isn't rocks he's after, it's bones and footprints. What do you call that, when they want to hunt in the desert and mountains after remains? "

" Undertaker," Tim suggested hopefully.

" No such thing, and don't get smart when I'm telling you interesting news. He's after prehistoric animals and people. He's a comical old badger; he hasn't got any money, he told me, but he wants some supplies and he's going to roam off up in the mountains alone and see what's there."

" Can't you ship him back on the next stage?

Maybe they've missed him by now," said Tim, with keen interest.

" But he ain't crazy, not a bit. He's all there. I sat and listened to him talk to Quinn, and Quinn was just pumping him to see if he was sane and safe, and he says the old man's all right."

Tim laughed. " I wonder if anybody ever pumped Quinn to find out if he was crazy or not."

" Crazy like an old fox," Sam said. " He knows more about the west than any man I ever met. He's travelled from the Arctic down to the Gulf. He knows the ways of every wild animal that ever existed."

" Sandy says he's just an old smokestack burning wind. Anyhow, I'm going along. I like these dates, Sam."

" Help yourself and bring in some more news when you're riding by." Sam went back behind the counter whistling, and Tim left with a good sized handful of dates. As she was mounting she saw Jim Quinn strolling up to the store, hatless, his hands deep in his pockets, his face twisted into wrinkles as if he were thinking deeply all the time. He pretended he never saw her, and went into the store, his old corncob pipe stuck in one corner of his mouth, unlit.

Tim ignored him loftily and rode around the square so she would have to pass by Mrs. Barney's on the way home. The big car stood in the back yard with its luggage removed, and she saw Margot standing on the front porch with Mrs. Barney's black kitten in her arms petting it.

" Hello," Tim called in friendly greeting as she rode by, but Margot did not seem to hear or see her. " Smarty," thought Tim. " Oh, very well, don't remember me if you don't want to, after I helped you and watered you all and everything. Just think you can drive into Frisbee with a governess and chauffeur and snub Katherine Campbell McLean. Next time I say hello to you, you'll know it."

She rode stormily back along the old wagon road with Chapo at a gallop, his ears laid back and his thin wiry legs taking the bumps like a sprinting jack rabbit.

CHAPTER III

It was not until the following morning that Tim felt like unbending with the boys after they had left her in the lurch Saturday. When they had returned in time for dinner, she had kept out of their way with a distant and lofty manner, and had refused to tell them one bit of her news even after Pablo had told them all about the big car and the strangers who had stopped at the ranch to ask the way to Frisbee.

But when they were all at breakfast Sunday morning Tim's eyes opened wider when she heard her father telling Tom that he had heard the Hayes-Roberts interests had sent out Chandler Thorpe, their best consulting engineer, to look over Frisbee properties.

"How long will he be out here, Father?" asked Tim eagerly.

"Quite a while, I expect. They take their time. His coming here at all means something interesting. I'd like to meet him because I've heard he's the best man they've got back east."

Mr. McLean spoke to Tom, but Tim leaned her chin on her palm, looking at him with indignant eyes from the foot of the long refectory table where she sat in her mother's place.

" Well," she said, " I hope he's better than the rest of the family. I liked Chester, the chauffeur, best. At least he was polite to a person. And if the whole family showed up this minute I wouldn't lift my finger to do a thing for them."

" What did they do to you, Fireworks? " asked Tom.

" And if you feel that way about them, why did you offer to ride all the way into town to show them the right road? " Neil demanded. " Pablo says you said you'd go before they even asked you."

Tim helped herself leisurely to more hot wheat cakes from Estrella's tray before replying. " I'm sure I don't see how this whole ranch would ever exist if it wasn't for Pablo. He never misses anything except work, and he sleeps all day with one eye half open like a horrid little brown lizard. Don't mind me, Estrella, you can't help it if he's your boy, and I love you just the same, especially your cakes."

Estrella smiled back at her with tender tolerance, and shuffled easily back to the kitchen over the tiled floor. But her father looked down at Tim keenly, his gray eyes that were so like her own, looking her through and through, as Tim always said.

"Did you meet any of the Thorpe outfit, daughter, when they came through?" he asked.

"I wasn't exactly introduced," Tim replied carefully, "but I suppose I might say I met them in a way. The governess is old and fat and French, and they call her Tumpy, and there is a boy named Dick and his sister is Margot. I just showed them the way to Mrs. Barney's, and I wish I'd told them to go to the National now where they wouldn't get a decent thing to eat."

"You've got such a sweet disposition. Why don't you like them? They must have done something to you. Go on and tell it; you know you will before you get through."

Tim balanced her cup of cocoa in her two hands, little fingers crooked, and elbows planted on the table as she looked over at Don with aggravating unconcern. She sipped the cocoa slowly, her eyes making half moons over the rim of the cup.

" Supposing you ask Sandy about them the next time you go to see him," she said.

" You wouldn't put your elbows on the table like that if Mother were home," Don retaliated. " Didn't she tell you to set us boys a good example in manners? "

Neil promptly planted his elbows on the table and sipped his cocoa the same way, but Don swung sideways so he could read the comic section that was spread out on the floor beside him. Tim regarded them all with supreme disapproval. Her father and Tom had both gone back to reading the Sunday papers which they had brought up from Oro the night before. Which was something else that went wrong when Mother was away, thought Tim. Sunday morning they all sat and read papers instead of getting acquainted as a happy family should around the breakfast table. She didn't mind Neil so much, because he was only twelve and what else could one expect of a boy that age, but Don was fifteen and her special pal, and he might at least look interested when she was trying to worry them by not telling all she knew about the Thorpes.

"Excuse me, please, Father," she said finally with extreme formality, and rose from her chair to stand with both feet planted on Don's comic section. "Oh, yes," she added, "Sam had a queer sort of a person asleep in his back room yesterday, Professor, Professor——"

"Dodo," suggested Don wrathfully. "Get off my paper, will you?"

"Darling, I'm *so* sorry." Tim moved about three inches to north to the top strip he was reading. "If you will put your newspaper on the floor you must expect accidents to happen. He's from Indiana, Father, and Jim Quinn's keeping one eye on him to make sure he's after bones and relics and not Jim."

"Katherine Campbell McLean, curb your tongue," warned Mr. McLean, even while his eyes twinkled. "Jim's all right and not afraid of any sheriff in disguise. Better not hang around listening to Sam's store gossip."

"Well then, Jim shouldn't pay so much attention to strange folks," said Tim. "He never works, just wanders around hunting trouble, and nobody knows where he came from or who he is, and I don't like him myself."

"Sandy says he's known him ever since he was a little fellow," Neil interrupted. "Jim likes to trail after gold strikes and that's how he came here, and then he just liked the climate and stayed on after the strike died out."

"Climate?" repeated Tim scornfully. "He liked Sallie Jane Owen's cooking, and he married her, and Sallie Jane's had to work and support them both ever since. I can't bear him. Every time I see him strolling around, I just wish he was hard at work on a rock pile. I'd love to sit and eat apples and watch Jim crack rock."

"If Jim's got his eye on anybody he's got good cause," Don said. "He'll keep your professor in sight till he finds out what he's out here for. Jim's a natural born detective. He used to be deputy sheriff once somewhere, he told us boys, and he's wise about mines too. He's done all sorts of gold digging, from Alaska down to here. He knew a man once who could tell where there was free gold just by walking over the ground and when he struck the right spot, he said

he felt goose flesh all over him. Something
chemical about him, Jim says, so his skin prickled
when he got near gold."

Everyone laughed, and Don added earnestly,
" All right, you can ask Sandy if it isn't so. And
Jim reads books too, and they swap, he and
Sandy."

" I suppose," Tim remarked, " if you found a
coyote reading one of Sandy's books, you'd give
him a clean bill of character. If I see the professor rambling around, I shall certainly tell
him all I know about Mr. Quinn, and warn him
not to tell all he knows."

The sleek brown head of Pablo appeared suddenly around the side of the porch door like a
sleepy salamander. " They go away last night together," he announced lazily. " I see them two
ride off along the Ridge 'bout sundown and go
down to the desert. Jim Quinn and some man
who not ride so good, no *savez* horse."

Tim stared at him resentfully. " Well, for
pity's sake, did you just find your tongue? Why
do you keep things to yourself till it's old stale
news? Why didn't you tell us this last night? "

Pablo pulled himself slowly together, and

stood up, stretching his arms widely and yawning. Then he strolled away from the house down
to the corral where Tim knew he'd just go to
sleep again in a shady spot under the pepper
trees.

"I don't believe him," Tom said flatly. "You
couldn't recognize anyone riding along the ridge
at that time."

"Yes, you could at sundown," Don answered,
squinting one eye as he looked out the door at
the high rim of the canyon opposite the ranch.
"You could see people and mules and horses up
there. They'd look like black cut-outs against
the red sky. I saw a coyote once at sundown
right up on that point yonder and you could tell
exactly what he was and which way he was standing."

Tim listened restlessly, longing to join in, but
still on her dignity. All at once she heard hoof-
beats down the road and hurried out of the house
to beat the boys in welcoming their regular Sunday morning caller, Dave Watson. He turned
his big bay horse in at the bar gate and slowed
down beside Tim, swinging out of the saddle and
offering her his big tanned palm with a friendly

grin, while he swept off his gray Stetson with the other in salute.

"Tim, how are you?" he said heartily. ".What's new?"

Tim smiled back at him with relief and confidence. Next to her father, she had more respect for Dave than anybody she knew. Beyond their own domain of McLean's Wash, only Dave Watson knew the desert and mountains just as they knew every little trail and rock in their canyon. Ever since she could remember, it had been his custom to stop at the ranch every other Sunday morning as he rode through on his way to visit his mother over in Frisbee. He was tall and lean and slow spoken. Tim always thought he looked like a soldier, but she never could find out what special war he'd ever been in. Sandy told her once he was sure Dave had been a Rough Rider, but when she tried to question the old ranger, he dodged details and laughed. "I always manage to show up where I'm needed most," he told her. To-day, she tackled him at once about whether he had seen anything of Jim Quinn and the old professor.

"Certainly did," said Dave cheerfully. "Met

Jim coming back this morning early. He said he'd been guiding some old man over the Ridge and started him on the right track across the desert to the Horseshoe. Told me to keep an eye out for him here and there because he didn't seem to have much sense of direction about him. Seemed well supplied, going out to hunt remains and relics for some museum, he told Jim; might be gone around a month."

" Oh, dear," sighed Tim, " there's another perfectly good mystery all gone to grass. I had it all planned for him to drift away into the desert after hidden gold and Jim would find out his secret and bury him deep. Nothing interesting ever happens in this place, Mr. Watson, nothing but school, and boys, and *enchilladoes*. We're going to have them again to-day. I love to eat dinner at Sandy's because you get plenty of frankfurters or boiled ham and beans and ginger ale. You do your own cooking, too, don't you?"

" Certainly do," said Dave, seriously. " You come up to my place on Lookout for dinner sometime with the boys, and I'll give you as fine a mess o' quail as you ever tasted."

" Expect me any time, but not with those

boys," Tim replied, striking an attitude of utter contempt. "They went to Sandy's without me yesterday, and we are not even on speaking terms."

"Don't you believe her, Dave, she did speak to me," Don broke in as they reached the front porch. "She couldn't resist it. She loves her little brothers so much, don't you, Timmie?"

"You ought to train them better," Dave said. "Here you're queen over this ranch while your mother's away, and they have to take orders whether they like it or not. Just you tell them that from me, and I'll back you up any time you need me. Just light a signal fire, Tim, and I'll come day or night."

"Hope you heard that, Don," Tim remarked pointedly, but presently she forgot all about her feud with the two boys, when Tom and her father strolled down to the corral with Dave to ask his opinion about Tom's pony, Buckskin. Tom was positive one of the boys had raced him down steep trails and sprung his knees because he stumbled every time he cantered now.

"It was not us that did that, Tom," protested Don. "We never ride him, do we, Timmie, but

Pablo does. He likes Buck better than his own pinto."

"I'd just like to catch him riding Buck," Tom said quietly. "I've told you youngsters to keep off my horse and I'm not going to have a lazy *cholo* breaking Buck's knees, that's all. He's got his own pony."

"Well, you can all pick on Pablo but he's all right just the same," Neil growled. "Gee, I don't see why he has to be the patsy on this ranch all the time. You lay everything on him, Tom, and I don't like it."

"You don't, Skeezicks, don't you?" Tom quizzed. "What do you know about it?"

"Because I rode your old horse myself." Neil stuck his fists deep in his pockets and shook his head firmly. He looked so comical in an old pair of Tom's corduroys belted-in almost double over a shirt of Don's, that they all had to laugh at him, and Neil slammed out hotly. "All right, you don't have to worry about his knees, either. It isn't his knees at all. He rolled down hill and got some bumps, that's all. So did I, and I won't ride your old sawhorse again. I'd hitch him up to a buggy first."

Tom made a dash, but Neil fled for the house and Don departed with his father and Dave, but Tim stayed with Tom while he felt Buckskin's slim legs up and down carefully.

" Mr. Watson never said a word, did he? " she asked.

" He wouldn't. He likes Pablo. Told me the Mexie saved his life once when he was cut off in a fire over in the mountains. Dave says he knows more about things than any ranger."

" Is Pablo half breed? "

" I guess so. Why? "

" Because you called him *cholo*."

" Most Mexies are half breeds, aren't they? "

" I don't know. I just wanted to be sure, because I'd love to ask Estrella all about her romance with an Indian if she did marry one. I think it would be terribly interesting. She's a grand old girl, know it, Tom, the way she puts up with all of us and goes around smiling no matter what happens. I think I'll forgive Pablo for not telling me the boys had gone and left me, and maybe I'll forgive them too. Sunday things seem so easy you feel you could forgive everybody, don't you? It's awfully tiresome anyway, not speaking to people when you're angry at them, you miss them so."

"Guess you miss being the only girl around here," Tom shot a quick look at her. "How's this new Thorpe girl? Maybe you'll get her for a girl friend."

"No, thanks," Tim answered flatly. "If you could just see her." She mimicked Margot's manner perfectly. "'Chester, will you see if we can get a drink of water?' Why couldn't she say to me pleasantly, 'Where's the well, old dear?' and we'd have been acquainted instantly."

"I wouldn't go too fast if I were you, Tim. I imagine that Dad wants to be good friends with her father."

"Why?" asked Tim indifferently. "Father knows a good deal more about mining around here than anybody does."

"Well, perhaps that's why he should know Mr. Thorpe," Tom told her. "Think it over. The Hayes-Roberts bunch aren't sending a man like that out to Frisbee for his health, you know."

Tim perched herself on the top rail of the corral, her forehead puckered into a frown. "They'd never send anybody unless they suspected there might be something worth hunting around here, is that what you mean?"

"I don't know anything about it," Tom said. "I just use my brain a little." He patted the pony's flank. "Go on, boy, you're all right."

Buckskin ambled down to the shady end of the corral and Tom went back to the house. Tim dropped from the rail and started after him, when all at once she saw the figure of Pablo stretched out flat on the ground along the side of the feeding shed, apparently sound asleep. She picked up a handful of pepper pods and threw them at him one by one until he raised his head from his crossed arms lazily and grinned at her, a sudden, good-natured smile like his mother's, his black eyes sparkling and white teeth flashing.

"I'll bet a cookie that you did spring Buck's knees and Neil just took the blame for you," Timmie said suspiciously. "You'd better watch out if Tom ever catches you at it."

"You think Tom can catch Cholo. He be like jack rabbit after coyote," drawled Pablo.

"Is that so, smarty? Wait till I tell Tom what you said."

Pablo rolled over and pointed at the branches

of the pepper tree over her head. " Tell mocking bird," he said, " maybe he talk little faster than you."

All at once the figure of Estrella appeared bearing down on them from the kitchen with two large flat baskets on her arms. " Come, Pablo," she called in her soft, musical voice, " where is the mama's little baby lizard, go pick-a mama much-a melon, much-a beans, much-a potato. Good boy, too much-a hot for the mama."

Pablo scowled blackly as he took the baskets and started off for the field with Tim singing after him teasingly, " Much-a hot, oh, much-a hot, little baby lizard!"

She danced back to the house after Estrella to hurry and dress for church, and twenty minutes later Miss Katherine Campbell McLean sat beside her father on the front seat of the roadster waving good-bye to Dave Watson as he rode ahead of them into Frisbee. Very dignified and properly dressed she looked, too, all in white, and clean and sweet as a mariposa lily.

She wondered whether she would see the Thorpes at church. If she did she'd make believe she didn't. Yet was that really right on

Sunday? Tim meditated seriously over it and decided she would bow ever so slightly if they did first, or even if they acted as if they would like her to speak to them. She wondered where Mrs. Thorpe was. Maybe they didn't have any mother at all, poor things, and here Tim relapsed into a long stretch of imagination over what a terrible thing it would be not to have a mother, so that by the time they reached St. Augustine's, she found herself stepping out right beside the Thorpe car, and smiled at them before she thought.

"Oh, there you are," said Margot. "Did you have a good ride yesterday? I wanted to come ever so much and Father said of course I might have gone when he came home, didn't you, dear?"

Mr. Thorpe turned around, and before Tim realized it, everyone was introduced and smiling and being very neighborly. They walked up the little stone flagged path to church, her father talking to Mr. Thorpe and Dick, with Don and Margot with her.

Tim thought serenely when she was seated in their pew the second from the chancel on the left side of the church, that Sunday certainly did do queer things to you. If you'd just relax and let it manage you, all the tangles of the week seemed to straighten out. And just as she was settling into the proper mood for the processional, she saw to her horror the shiny inquisitive head of Don's pet black lizard poke itself out of the side pocket of his new gray coat. It was no use warning Don, the lizard would surely escape, so she reached over and took it firmly by the neck and walked with dignity out of church holding Squeetaw at arm's length.

Margot and Dick saw her and smiled delightedly, but Tim left him in the pocket of the car. "If he gets away from there, it's his own affair," she thought philosophically, and went back just in time to walk slowly behind Mr. Maynard and the choir boys while they sang,

"Fling out the banner, let it float,
Seaward and skyward ——"

Here Tim caught Margot's inquiring glance and rolled her own eyes in the direction of the car to let her know Squeetaw had been safely banished from service.

CHAPTER IV

ALL through the next week of school-days Tim was divided in interest between catching glimpses of Margot and stopping in for mail every day so she could gossip with Sam and see if he had any news of the old professor. The only gratifying thrill she got was finding out that Jim had only come back after his own outfit. Monday he had ridden out of Frisbee over the Ridge route to join the professor, and Sam seemed very dubious over the unselfishness of Jim's motives.

"I think he got wind of something from the old boy," he told Timmie seriously. "Probably pumped him until he made him tell him the real object of his trip out here, and then made him think he needed experienced company. That's what I think privately. Maybe the professor's after bones and maybe he ain't. There's gold mostly anywhere out this way if you keep looking for it more or less. Personally I'd rather hunt for black gold. Know what that is, Tim?"

" Certainly I know, oil," retorted Tim.

" Oil it is, and how, plenty much oil, gushing millions for you and you don't have to bend your back and dig to get at it. I've done my bit in gold mines and I'd a heap rather have it flowing out at me, yes, ma'am." Sam went to work the gas pump for some passing tourists and came back wiping his hands on his store apron.

"Do you believe there's any real gold left around here, Sam?" asked Tim musingly.

Sam leaned his elbows on the top of the glass show case and regarded the bread and cake inside observantly before he answered. " Frankly, since you ask me, I do not. It ain't the right sort of drift for gold, but you never can tell about oil. Dig anywhere you like out west and there she gushes. I loaned ten dollars to a man once who came through here on his way to California, broke and busted. Four years later that man came in here with a big roaring fancy car standing right out by that pump, and he planted five hundred dollars down on this very counter, and he says, ' Brother, you staked me when I didn't have a cent, and there's my come back.' He'd turned rich out of oil, nothing but oil, and was on his way back east to stupefy all his folks who hadn't believed in him."

"Oh, Sam, wasn't that wonderful?" Tim sighed. She loved to listen to Sam's stories. Sam nodded his head, pushed back the green shade from his eyes, and prepared to gratify an eager listener, but all at once Tim saw three horses go by out in the street with the Thorpes riding, and in a flash she was out and on Chapo, dashing after them as they headed toward the canyon.

When she passed them at a gallop the children's ponies shied sideways and tried to race after her, but she reached the ranch ahead of them. Don and Neil were nowhere to be found, so she watched eagerly by herself for the Thorpes to turn in at the bar gate, but instead they rode on by and only waved to her as she stood waiting on the porch. Somehow it seemed hard to get really acquainted with them, Tim thought, her longing for a girl chum fighting with her pride. Margot always smiled at her, but they had not stopped at the ranch again, and of course Tim felt she couldn't go to Mrs. Barney's to see them without an invitation. So there you were,

she decided; you could go just so far with some
things, and when they didn't happen, you had to
just wait and trust to luck. After a while Don
came into the house, grimy and hot after a ride,
and she told him about it.

"If you'd get acquainted with her brother it
would help."

"Don't want to," replied Don briefly. "He
looks too dumb."

"Well, you can get that right out of your
mind because he isn't one bit dumb."

"Is that so?" Don looked at her flushed face
with interest. "How do you know so much?"

"I heard him talking to Sam one day in the
store. He's travelled all over the world. They've
lived in South Africa and India and Australia.
Their mother is dead, and Mr. Thorpe takes the
two youngsters with him everywhere he goes,
with Tumpy to teach them. After this year,
though, they have to go back to England to
school."

"How did you drag all that out of him,
Nosy?"

"I didn't, I say; Sam did. Sam could take
the Goddess of Liberty and make her tell him

her middle name, I believe. Anyway, I don't blame him for being interested. I think it's nice and friendly to be sociable with people. It makes them feel at home. Margot Thorpe always looks lonesome to me."

"You mean you're fed up on us boys and wish you had a girl out here on the ranch."

"What if I do? Goodness knows you leave me out of everything, Don McLean. You knew perfectly well I wanted to ride over to Sandy's with you Saturday, and I am going there next Saturday all by myself, and the week after I'm going to have dinner on Lookout at Dave Watson's, he said so, without you two boys trailing along."

"You'll have to use an airplane to get up on top of Lookout where he lives," chuckled Don. "Why don't you ask Margot to go up with you, give her a real wild west thrill. Or trot her out to Sandy's. You know he'd just fall over with joy to see a couple of girls ride up without fair warning."

"I think I'll do it." Tim warmed up instantly to the suggestion, quite contrary to what Don had expected she would do. "I'll go over to

Mrs. Barney's to-day and ask her if she'd like to go with me."

"You'd better not," warned Don. "I was only kidding, Tim. She's never ridden in the desert and she'd keel over riding out there nine miles."

"Dear child, she's lived in the Sahara and ridden camels in caravans," replied Tim loftily. "Our little dab of desert would look like a sand pile to her." Tim surprised herself immensely the way she took Margot's part and silenced Don, and late that afternoon she coaxed Estrella into saying she needed baking powder at once, and rode into Frisbee for it. But after buying it, she steered Chapo over to Mrs. Barney's and rode in the side way up to the kitchen door where the pony planted his forefeet on the top step and waited with his nose pressed against the screen door.

"Hello, Sallie Jane!" called Timmie.

"Hello, Timmie." Sallie left her cooking to come to the door with an apple for Chapo and a smile for Tim. The pony nibbled and nuzzled at it on her outstretched palm, twisting his neck like a dog worrying a bone as he tried to get at it around his bit. "How's things in the canyon?"

"Fine. Heard from Jim?"

"No," Sallie answered easily. "It's hardly time, you know. They were making for the Horseshoe, but I'm never worried about Jim. He knows every trail in those mountains; that's why Professor Peck asked him to go along with him."

"Oh, yes," Tim looked relieved. "Well, I hope they get back all right. Seems as if everybody's interested in them now. Where's Margot Thorpe, do you know, Sallie?"

"They left here yesterday."

"Left?" exclaimed Tim. "Where could they go? I just saw them all out riding right after school. I didn't go to-day. The car got two punctures and we all gave out trying to fix them."

"I only mean they all left here. But they've taken over the Garden House. I understand Mr. Thorpe's looking for a sort of dude ranch where the children can make believe they're roughing it. Mr. Barney tried to sell him the old Lopango place but they didn't want to go so far away from Frisbee. See anything of Sandy lately?"

"No, but I'm going to ride over Saturday."

"You are?" Sallie looked at her eagerly. "Say, Timmie, will you just ask him to specially keep an eye out for Jim for me? He said he was going past the Splinter."

"Sure I'll tell Sandy. Good-bye." Tim smiled as she turned Chapo back to the street. Just the same, she thought, Jim and the professor had not taken the road past the Splinter, they had gone over the Ridge route that led to the short cut to the mountains across the desert. Sallie didn't know this, so why should she tell her and give her something to worry about? Jim did know his way around, but why should he tell Sallie Jane he was going one way when he must have known he was going another?

Tim puzzled over it, and resolved to ask Sandy's cool, calm opinion when she saw him Saturday.

The Garden House stood on the only hill in Frisbee, half a hill really, for it was like a footstool placed before the rising wall of rose and violet tinted mountains. Just now they looked pretty barren and dusty. Tim thought as she rode along how much better it was over in the canyon, and how glad she would be when school let out in June. Margot and Dick were lucky they only had a governess, no regular hours, no exams, nothing to worry about. She wondered just how much they knew and how far they were ahead of her. Probably they had their lessons when they were travelling just as she did at school, lessons de luxe in a private car, maybe a drawing-room.

One of Tim's pet ambitions was to ramble around the country in a drawing-room. She loved to stand on the station platform when the eastern limited trains whizzed by and sometimes they would slow down so she could get a peek into the drawing-rooms or the diner. If she could ever be sure she would ride on those trains, she often thought, life would look more interesting ahead. And here Margot and Dick Thorpe had probably spent a large share of their lives going about that way or on ocean liners.

She halted Chapo before the Garden House, and slid from the saddle with a final warning to the pony to behave himself and not start chewing shrubbery the minute her back was turned.

Then she straightened the red silk tie on her favorite pongee shirt, hitched up her brown suede belt and walked up the flagged path to the front door, looking rather well, she thought, even if her tan linen trousers were creased from riding. But just as she was half-way she heard a hail from the driveway that curved around the house to the back yard. Margot's head stuck out from under a new roadster as she called to Tim to come on over, and Dick's legs clad in blue overalls appeared just beyond her. It was a re-assuring sight, Tim thought. She lost her company manners instantly and ran to join them.

" Hello," said Dick in muffled tones. " Know anything about a car? "

" Everything," Tim said. "What's the matter?"

" It won't go. We got it for Margot's birth-day ——"

" You mean I got it," protested Margot. " You never let me use your rifle or run your motor boat."

" He'll have a grand time trying to run a motor boat out here," Tim laughed. " I think you're working at the wrong end of that. Get out from underneath and let me try something."

The two wriggled out and stood up, hot and dusty and greasy, while Tim got in the car. As she had suspected, the starter was jammed, so she threw the car in gear and told Dick and Margot to rock it backward and forward slowly. Then the starter clicked itself into place. Dick stared at her in admiration.

"Thanks," he said, "that wasn't half bad. I should have known how to do it myself. I've driven a lot, haven't I, Margot?"

"You're a crazy driver," Margot said calmly, "that's why I got the car and you didn't. Do you like to drive, Tim?"

"Hate it," Tim answered heartily. "I only like to ride a horse. Want to go out with me Saturday on the desert? I'm going to visit an old friend of mine."

"I'd love to. Wonder if Tumpy'd die, Dick, if I went. Who is your friend, Tim?"

"Name's Sandy," said Tim carelessly. "I have never found out what the rest of it is."

"That's the old fellow the storekeeper pointed out to us, Margot, and said he was a desert rat."

Tim looked at Dick in a way anyone who knew

her would have considered a fair danger signal,
but Dick failed to get the warning.

" I don't think you'd better go, Margot."

" You don't know anything about Sandy,"
Tim began deliberately. " It would be just like
Sam to hand you out that stuff about Sandy or
anyone he thought interesting, just to give you
folks a dash of wild west life. But Sandy's got
more education than Sam ever dreamt of. He
comes from a very well known society family in
New York, that's why he won't tell people his
last name, he doesn't want his family looking
him up and being a lot of trouble to him. He
says he's all fed up on New York, and he loves
the desert and the mountains and his books.
Wait till you see his place, Margot. He's fascinating to me because ——" Tim tried to think
of a good one that would impress Dick, " because
he's original and very mysterious."

Margot wanted to go and said she'd try to get
her father to consent, but Dick said doggedly,
" I don't think you should ride way off into the
desert with only a girl with you."

" Don't mind him, Tim, I think Father will
say yes."

"He will not." Dick looked so dignified and positive that Tim longed to do anything to disconcert him.

"Oh, well," she said carelessly, "I suppose I'd better ask Sandy first anyway, whether he'd let me bring you out. He's very particular about whom he meets."

She strolled away toward the street, Margot following her. "Don't mind anything Dick says to you, he's just a perfect little brute like most boys. I'd love to ride with you, and I'll ask Father to-night if I may and let you know. I've been looking off at the desert ever since we arrived, wishing I could get out into it. Tumpy's just as silly as Dick over my riding alone, but we'd be all right together. I'll leave a card at the post office for you, Tim, surely."

"Any time," Tim told her as if it did not matter in the least, and she mounted Chapo and dug her heels into his sides until he bounded forward down the street. Margot watched her out of sight admiringly, and went back to Dick.

"Why did you act like that? I like her," she said.

Dick did not answer for a minute; he got in the

car, and drove it into the garage, and came back
frowning. " She treats us like a couple of sticks,
as if we didn't know anything about horses or
deserts or her old ranches, and she's never been
out of this place in her life."

" Then why do you get all fussed up over what
she says? You're angry with her just because
she knew how to fix the car, and you didn't.
And she rides like an Indian."

" Anyone could ride in a rocking-chair saddle
like she's got. I'd like to see her on a real hunting saddle; she'd hit the stars," Dick retorted
gruffly, and he strode away, his head high. Margot stood looking after him curiously. She had
never seen Dick bothered over any girl before.
She called after him teasingly:

" Tim can ride without any saddle at all."

" On a clothes horse," Dick shouted back.
" Don't talk to me about her, I can't bear her."

Margot smiled slowly to herself as if she had
just made a very interesting discovery. In all
her years of closest companionship with Dick, he
had never noticed any girl but herself. He was
always terribly aloof with them and refused to
get acquainted, because he said they were all

silly. Certainly he had never allowed one to
worry him or get him angry like this, and Margot decided it only meant one thing, he was
jealous of Tim, of her riding and knowing how
to fix the car, and her familiarity with the desert
and wilderness that they both longed to penetrate. Dick must think Tim was interesting, or
he'd never stop to notice her.

She followed after him into the house. "Dick,"
she called. "I want to speak to you."

"I'm going to bathe," he said shortly, half-
way up the staircase. "I'm filthy from that car."

"Do you really mind if I ride with Tim Saturday?"

"Just you try it. Father and Tumpy would
be delighted to have you call on a desert rat,
wouldn't they?" He grinned back at her over
the railing. "You might manage Father, but I
can manage Tumpy."

"Wait until you want to drive my car,"
warned Margot. "Now I know you are jealous
of Tim, but I like her."

There came the sound of a slamming door up-
stairs, and silence, profound, shutting off all
argument over Timmie.

CHAPTER V

VERY early Saturday morning Tim left the ranch and started off for Sandy's place. She ate breakfast with Tom and her father around six-thirty, hoping to get away before the two younger boys woke up, and had ridden happily off on Chapo for four or five miles when she heard a long-drawn hail, and turning around, she was surprised to see Don racing after her on Dusty, his own particular mouse-colored bronco.

" Now just why did you have to come along? " she asked indignantly when he reached her and drew up alongside. " I wanted to go alone to-day to see Sandy, and not have either one of you boys tagging along after me."

" Can't a person ride out on this whole desert without getting permission from you? " Don queried lazily. " I promised Sandy I'd bring him something he wanted to-day sure, so I had to come, didn't I? "

" I don't believe you." Tim looked him over with scorn. " You'd make up anything to tell.

You just followed after me to worry me. I know you, Don, you're just as full of curiosity as an old hound pup, nosing 'round everywhere. What did you promise Sandy you'd bring out to him, honest, now?"

"Fish hooks," said Don innocently. "Don't you believe me? Look here."

He dug in his pants pocket and pulled out a small, flat whittled-out piece of wood with four new fish hooks stuck carefully into it. "Believe me now?"

"I don't see how he can go fishing just the same. He's about twenty-two miles from real running water."

"Going south," Don protested. "Sandy's planning something else. He asked us boys to go on a fishing trip with him clear over the range up to Bluewater Lake. He says he'll take us up there for two weeks in vacation and nobody knows where it is but Indians and himself. Where's Margot Thorpe? I thought you said she was coming with you to-day."

"Her father and Tumpy are afraid Sandy's a dangerous person, and she might get lost besides, with only me to take care of her." Tim's eyes

were fixed ahead of her on the shifting colors
over the desert, now long waves of violet that
changed, as you gazed, into rose and gold as the
sun arched higher; then the mountains ahead
seemed to hold every shade of rose and pink and
opalescent red as the mists cleared away.
Gophers scudded ahead of them racing for cover,
or sat up outside their holes like little sentinels,
staring until suddenly they too took fright, and
almost turned somersaults in their rush to hide
away.

They rode down from the mesa and came out
on the level dusty land that stretched north and
west as far as they could see until the desert
blended into the amethyst haze of the Horseshoe
range. The sagebrush was past its best bloom
and the flowers were mostly gone except for a
few last poppies that shone like flecks of bright
gold on the brown earth. Here and there a
cactus stood out like a strange living figure on
the waste land, with one or two arms upraised as
if in perpetual surprise at something. Tim always thought that at night they looked like giants.

They followed the narrow wagon road from
the canyon as it cut across the desert following

the old Indian trail. The ponies made short work of the nine miles over to Sandy's, even slowing down part of the way, and they drew up before his little straggling makeshift shack with its two lean-tos screened in from mosquitoes and flies, and the strange enclosures back of it under the big cottonwood.

Sandy had his own names for these. He said they were built on as afterthoughts as the need came for them. One was the Moon Parlor. Most people had sun parlors, but he needed a moon parlor because he liked to sleep out of doors at night with just the sky overhead, and so he had built a little platform up on posts and boarded it half-way up, then on four poles at the corners he had stretched chicken wire and over this again, mosquito netting. Inside was Sandy's couch and a little table with some books on it, and an oil lamp, tin, with a handle and reflector.

About twenty feet away was Old Maid's Retreat, a corral where Connie lived, a fretful old gray mare who was pensioned for life by Sandy because he had travelled west on her long ago. The corral had to be fenced off into two sections since Connie could not abide the two little burros,

Tony and Cleo, named for Anthony and Cleopatra. These were Tim's favorites and she always made a point of letting them know she was visiting Sandy. They were patient and gentle, listening with only an occasional blink of their wide eyes when Sandy scolded them, or Powder barked at their heels when they were on the road.

Powder was another sort of citizen in Sandy's desert domain. He was mostly Airedale and had been presented when he was a puppy to Sandy by the McLean children in token of their undying esteem and friendship. He had been the liveliest member of a new family belonging to Maggie, Neil's pet, so Powder often felt the home call and would travel by himself all the long way back to the ranch to play around a few days with his own particular people. Sandy didn't mind at all. He said it showed a fine streak of loyalty in the pup, but when it came to Powder trailing off to hunt rabbits all by himself, that was another question. Whenever he had hunted rabbits Powder's whole manner changed from a frisky, care-free dog to a straggling culprit, stealing back to the shack to hide from Sandy's accusing eye.

He was in disgrace to-day, curled up under the long wash bench by the door with a depressed and penitent look in his appealing brown eyes as he looked eagerly out at the children.

Sandy sat tilted back on an old wooden chair, his feet on the rounds, reading a book. He was somewhere around sixty with gray curly hair that grew on his head in points like Pantaloon, and a thin gray moustache with long ends like a mandarin. In spite of his worn old trousers and ragged shirt, there was an unmistakable air of family pride and dignity about Sandy. He rose and greeted them with cordial pleasure, shook hands with them both and showed Tim his book, " The Lady of the Lake."

" Ever read it? Scott? " he asked.

" I think so. We have to read him in school," said Tim. " ' The stag at eve,' and ' Charge, Chester, Charge, on, Stanley, on.' "

" You've got him right," Sandy told her gravely. " My favorite poet. I et my breakfast around six, so I've been sort of easin' along ever since. Did you bring me those fish hooks, Don? "

" Didn't I tell you he asked for them, Tim? " Don grinned as he took the crushed envelope from his pocket and dug out the fish hooks stuck in the piece of wood. " Here you are."

" What are you going to catch, Sandy? " Tim asked curiously. Sandy winked at Don.

" This is my own invention for catching gophers," he said. " I'm going to bait these with salt pork and fool 'em."

" Gophers don't eat salt pork from fish hooks," Tim remarked calmly. ".Why don't you let Powder chase them? "

" Can't fool her, can we, Don? " Sandy said. " All right, ma'am. We may go away fishing before long, soon as vacation comes. I don't suppose there's another white man in this part of the States 'cepting me that knows where Bluewater Lake is. It is an absolutely hidden body of water behind that range of mountain you see yonder." He stepped inside the shack and hid the fish hooks carefully behind the row of books on the narrow shelf by the fireplace.

" How do you get to it? " asked Tim.

" I couldn't tell anybody else how to get there to save my life." Sandy came out of the shack scratching his head thoughtfully. " It's sort of instinct, I suppose. Powder's like that, he can steer himself anywhere at all just by his nose and instinct, and my nose is most as long as his."

"Why don't you let Powder chase the gophers away?" asked Tim.

"He won't kill them, he's too tender hearted. Do you know that dog has a whole class of young gophers he's teaching out yonder. Yes, ma'am. Every morning at sunrise he trots down below those cottonwoods and you can find him there sitting like a judge with a circle of gophers around him listening to him tell them the story of the man in the moon." Sandy's gray eyes twinkled as he caught the intent half credulous look in the children's faces. Then Tim laughed with delight as she always did over his stories. He looked at her with a frown. "Don't believe it, eh? Why do you suppose all dogs bay at the moon? They lift their heads and send up a salute to someone they know is up there, and the gophers are afraid of dogs because they know about the moon."

Don sauntered away toward a spot where an old rusty cook stove stood underneath a tent-fly. Sandy called this place his Banquet Hall and he grinned after Don as he saw him lean over and sniff at the two big covered iron pots that were cooking away on top of the stove.

"I'll have dinner around eleven, he's good an' hungry now," he promised. "Got boiled ham and beans and I'm going to make hot biscuit to go with them. Can't beat that much, can you? I told that boy if he'd bring me out fish hooks I'd dig out a couple of bottles of ginger ale for him."

"That's awfully nice of you, Sandy," Tim said, suddenly remembering her promise to Sallie. "Have you seen anything of an old man and Jim Quinn? They've got a couple of horses and two pack mules and they're bound for the mountains."

"Yep," Sandy told her placidly. "Found their tracks past the Splinter a few days ago. I could have told them they was going to get lost over there just as sure as I'm a foot high. There ain't but one trail through that range for thirty miles, and Jim knows that's the truth as well as I do, but he don't know the trail and I do. Even Dave Watson don't know that trail. I know every square foot of land in those mountains. I've gone up and explored for my own satisfaction every last canyon and every foot of wilderness, me 'n Powder, and there ain't any way to get through that range by foot or horseback 'ceptin' you go through the door in the mountain. Every canyon ends in a blind blank wall of rock a squirrel couldn't climb up. And they're all sproutin' rattlesnakes thick as grass. I've seen 'em myself."

"Professor Peck said he was going out to hunt for prehistoric remains and relics of animals before the flood, and cave people too," said Tim thoughtfully.

"Ain't he the ambitious old dodo? He won't find any, will he, Sandy?" Don called. "Say, when will dinner be ready? I'm starved."

"He'll find 'em if the snakes don't get him first," Sandy said encouragingly. "Stick around, Don, it's most done. Just sniff at it and work up a really good appetite. Let's sit out in the shade and talk."

They followed him around to the Sun Parlor and Broadway where a long wooden table was set under the big cottonwood and a long homemade wooden bench placed before it. An old armchair with the cane seat half broken in was at the head of the table, Sandy's accustomed place, but to-day he waived honors and offered it to Tim with a gallant gesture.

"Ladies first," he said grandly. "It's going to be 119 in the shade before it lets up to-day. You know I never need calendars or thermometers or clocks. I can tell time and days and temperatures by the sun and plants. Look at that creepin' shadow. It's twice again as far around as it was this time yesterday. I got a sun clock all marked out with sticks and stones, ever see it? Flat on the ground out back of the shack. All I have to do is glance out my window and see what time it is. If the sun ain't shining, I get back like an old hedgehog in my hole, and wait till I can see my shadow, then I go outdoors again."

"You are wonderful, Sandy." Tim sat with her two feet planted on the top rung of the chair, her chin on her palms and her elbows on her knees as she listened seriously. "You are much better than the judge or sheriff or a minister. They're wise, but you know that what you're talking about is right from personal experience, not just studying."

"Well, I just use my brain," Sandy said mod-

estly. " It's what it's there for. Take Jim Quinn
for instance. You and I both know Jim never
went trailing after that professor hoping to see
some new bones pop out of the ground. He's
suspicious the professor ain't telling strictly the
truth."

" Didn't I say so, Tim!" Don exclaimed.
" They're after gold."

" No, you didn't say so," Tim replied calmly,
" at least, not to me."

" But Jim's talked about gold a lot to us boys.
He believes there's plenty and he says the Indians know where it is."

Sandy lit his pipeful of tobacco slowly.
" Every white man has said that identical thing
ever since they came west. It just don't mean
nothing at all, and when Jim Quinn says it, it
means even less."

" But I believe it, Sandy," protested Tim.

" So do I," added Don.

Sandy glanced in surprise at the two stubborn,
eager young faces and shook his head.

" If they've gone hunting for gold in the
Horseshoe, they're done for. They won't never
come back."

"Oh, poor Sallie," Tim cried. "She'll die if anything happens to Jim."

"I think," Sandy continued calmly, "that they're lost right this minute because I followed their tracks as far as I could and they headed due north from the Splinter. Looks to me like Jim has been finding out some of my secrets for himself, but if he thinks he's going to pass through that range through the door in the mountain, he's missed his calculations."

"What's the door in the mountain?" Tim demanded. "I never heard of that before, did you, Don?"

"Nor nobody else in this generation," Sandy replied. "I came out west here when I was a very young man and things were wild. Outlaws and Indians and what not running around loose far as the eye can see. And I made friends with them all by keeping my mouth shut and my eyes open. Strange as it may seem, them fish hooks have got something to do with the door in the mountain because an old Indian whose life I saved out in the desert ——"

"How, Sandy?" asked Tim eagerly. "Don't skip, tell it all."

" He had been in a fightin', shootin', running scrape with a mess of other Indians, and left for dead beside his dead pony. I happened to come along and I saw his hand sticking up out of the sand kind of, and I saw it wasn't a dead man's hand. The finger nails were pink not blue, and I pulled him out and slung him across my saddle and brought him home with me, and took quite a fancy to him the way you will to anything alive that you save."

" Where is he now? " asked Don.

" He's really dead now, but he almost turned into a white man. He gave up prowlin' around and settled down in Frisbee, married a nice little Mexican girl ——"

" Oh, Sandy, was her name Estrella? " asked Tim. " Wouldn't that be marvelous if she turned out to be his wife? She married an Indian and Pablo is their son."

" I couldn't vouch for that," Sandy replied carefully. " I wouldn't go so far as to say which Mexican girl he married or what her name was. It's a long time ago, but before he died he told me the secret of the door in the mountain and also how to go fishing in Bluewater Lake whenever I wanted to. He was the gratefullest Indian I ever saw."

"Have you ever really seen it? What does it look like, Sandy?" Tim edged her chair nearer and hugged her knees until she looked like a half closed jack knife. Sandy gazed away from the shack and little corral and outbuildings to the high rim of distant mountains scalloped against the northern sky, his eyes half closed and keen.

"You can ride for days and days the way I did, hunting for it," he said. "And even if you've seen it once, still you may never find the way up to it, or locate it again. But it's there. I've seen it myself on a clear day and once I found it, just as he would, but the whole place was alive with rattlesnakes and I got away with my life. Just the same I picked up a piece of gold that would make any prospector's mouth water. Want to see it?"

Tim could hardly believe her ears, he asked it so carelessly. "Why, we'd love to, Sandy, if it isn't too much trouble," she said, gasping a little and fanning herself. Sandy assured them it wasn't a bit of trouble, he was delighted to show it to them, and he got up and ambled leisurely back to the shack. Tim stared at Don and he at her with wide, questioning eyes.

" Do you believe it? " she whispered.

" Sure," said Don. " He knows what he's talking about. And I'm going to find it."

" Rattlesnakes? "

" I'll get Dave to show me how to burn them out. He says after a forest fire, you won't see a rattlesnake nor any other snake for three years. It kills the live ones and cooks the eggs."

" Hush, here he comes," whispered Tim. Sandy came up holding a small wooden box in his hand with a sliding cover. Inside, packed in cotton, was a curiously shaped piece of gold.

" Looks like chewed gum only gold colored, doesn't it? " Don said, when Sandy lifted it out on the palm of his hand for them to look at and examine.

" Pick it up," he told them generously, " handle it, bite it, it's the real thing, free gold. I saw it shining at my feet as I was hot footin' it down the gulch away from those snakes, and I stooped down and picked it out. Must have been a river through that gulch some time hundreds of years ago, it's all rocks now, a dandy summer resort for the rattlers. Can't get into the gulch at all on a horse or burro, have to stick to a crazy trail along the side that's half washed away and the rest of it crumbling. But you can see for yourself, it's gold, ain't it?"

"Who do you suppose put the door in the mountain or tried to get at the gold?" asked Tim, thrilled as she held the queerly shaped nugget on her hand. "Indians or Mexicans?"

"Farther back than either, I'd say," Sandy said. "Spanish maybe. That door's made of wood like beams crisscrossed and clamped with iron, 'bout two feet thick."

"How do you know if you've never been on the other side of it, Sandy?" persisted Tim.

"Don't get too inquiring," answered Sandy. "I never tell all I know. Put it back in the box and you can put it away for me if you like. Stick the box under the mattress at the head of my bed. When I come up I'll put it where it goes."

Tim balanced the box on her hand carefully as if it had contained a crown jewel. "I think you're splendid to trust us like this with your secret, Sandy," she said.

Sandy grinned back at her over his shoulder as

he started for the Banquet Hall to take up dinner. " It ain't my secret. It's the rattlers'," he said. " Hurry up, and come to dinner. The beans are ready by now, and I'll dig out the ginger ale. And don't let your mind run on gold and things mysterious. You don't see me hunting for it, do you? No, ma'am. Books and sunshine for me, and peace of mind. While you're up there, you might bring down my old spy-glass on top of the shelf over the back door. When I first got it, I used to spend days sitting up on top of the Splinter scanning the mountains trying to locate that fool door, it got so on my mind."

" Oh, Sandy," Tim hesitated, and looked at Don who nodded his head at her encouragingly. " Would you loan us the spy-glass just for about a week? We'd take awfully good care of it."

"Yes, you would, and you'd fall down from the Splinter and crack your two necks before you got through. No, you can't borrow it." He started off toward the Banquet Hall with Powder at his heels, and Tim waited until he was out of hearing before she said:

" Don, he's afraid we'll find it."

"He knows we can't or he'd never have told us," retorted Don.

He followed Sandy, and Tim went up to the shack, thinking hard all the way. She placed the little box where Sandy had told her, under the corner of the mattress at the head of his bed, and found the spy-glass covered with dust on the crowded shelf over the back door. But when she tried to adjust it herself, everything was blurred before it, and she gave up. Don's whistle hailed her, and she hurried back to join them at the long table under the cottonwood where Sandy presided before a big dish of baked beans with boiled ham around them. Don opened up the ginger ale, and Tim, with great care, took the pan of biscuits out of the oven.

"I didn't even see you put these in," she said when she came back with them. "I'll bet you had them all mixed and rising ready to pop in, didn't you, Sandy?"

"I never give my methods away," said Sandy with dignity. "I may tell you the true facts, but I don't believe in trading methods. I got my own way of making biscuit, and it works out right. Did you bring the spy-glass with you?"

Tim laid it before him on the table. " But I tried to see through it, and couldn't."

" I'll show it to you after dinner," he promised, " and maybe I'll walk back with you, or ride Tony as far as the Splinter, and show you the queerest thing in this whole country, if it's clear enough to see it to-day."

" Sandy, you mean—oh, you wouldn't! " exclaimed Tim.

" I never promise what I can't do. Eat your dinner and forget gold and hopes. I can tell you one thing, I've been so starved that I'd have given all the gold in the world for one plate of beans like this."

CHAPTER VI

AFTER they finished dinner Sandy obligingly adjusted the telescope and showed Tim and Don how to rest it mariner fashion on the curve of their left arm while they looked through it.

"Which mountain is it?" asked Tim as she moved the telescope from side to side trying to focus it at the same time on the distant range. "It just looks like one long wall from here."

"Well, it's sort of hazy to-day." Sandy squinted one eye judicially and pointed over her shoulder. "There's the Splinter yonder. Now get that first, then move the instrument to the right and it's the first high elevation eastward in the Horseshoe range."

"I can't find it." Tim gave up the telescope to Don. "I don't see why they call these mountains anyway. They're just big hills, Margot says. She's seen the Alps and Rockies and Himalayas too."

"Who's this has been talking against my

range?" asked Sandy with dignity. "Them yonder are perfectly good mountains, and I've seen the Rockies and High Sierras, and while they may appear to be snow capped and otherwise dressed up, they ain't a mite more dangerous than those yonder, not as much, I'd say, come to think of rattlesnakes and danger from starvation. Who said this anyhow?"

"Margot Thorpe, a sort of a friend of mine. She just came out from the east, and she's really English, and she's got a brother Dick. You'd like them all right, Sandy, and she didn't mean anything probably, she was just judging from appearances."

"Bring her along some day, and I'll meet her," Sandy replied blandly, "but caution her not to call my range plain hills. It's a wonder she didn't say foothills and be done with it. I'm going to ride over with you youngsters and let you take a look through my glass from the Splinter. You go along and get your ponies because it's time we started along. It gets pretty blowy out here along about three or four o'clock these spring days."

Sandy had nothing more to say as they rode

along the dusty wagon trail that led from his shack across the desert toward the Splinter. Tim hummed to herself as she rode. It was a beautiful day and the desert was a patchwork of brilliant flowers, brilliant yellow like sprinkled gold where the poppies grew, and right next would be a great blanket of heavenly blue where the lupines lifted their bells. The Splinter stood up out of the radiant sun-swept distance like a sore thumb, Sandy said. It was a great jagged mass of strange conglomerate rock with straggling patches of sage and cactus clinging to it here and there, and a steep and narrow path winding around and around up to the summit, and worn by other feet than white men's from long ago days.

"I was coming along here one moonlight night," said Sandy, "and I just felt sort of uneasy like someone was hidden away and looking at me. And I got my gun out in my hand and when I came abreast of the Splinter way up there on the tip-top I saw a coyote sitting down as calm and collected as a big hound pup, and watching me. His eyes blazed away like fire, and he watched me clear out of sight, but I didn't

fire nor try to scare him off. He was having too
good a time all by himself."

They left the ponies at the base of the rock
although Tim said she knew she could ride Chapo
clear up to the top any time she wanted to. Once
they reached the summit, Sandy took his bearings
as he said, from the slant of the sun's rays already
spreading out fanwise in the west. The children
followed his line of vision as he pointed due north
at the dip in the mountain range opposite them.

" There you can see it," he said. " You'd have
to travel out here at high noon as I told you, and
stand on the north side down there, and wait till
the shadow of the rock pointed due north and if
you could follow it like a bird, you'd come right
out at the mountain with the door in it, right bang
at the foot of the identical canyon that leads up
to it. There ain't any special name for it and
that makes it confusing, but the Indian that first
told me about it, took me over here and showed
me how to get to it just as I'm showing you now.
High noon at the Splinter, then follow the
shadow right to its extreme point on the ground.
Lie down and get a good squint at it, and you'll
see that it certainly does point to one particular

mountain over in the range. Plain as the nose on your face once you know how to locate it. Old time scouts and prospectors put a good deal more reliance on a good shadow by the sun than they did in clocks or compasses."

"But it's a good sized mountain," Tim said. "Even if you got across the desert to it, maybe the door would be hidden by bushes or trees."

"Probably it is by now," Sandy agreed heartily. "But if you ever do get as far as that blind canyon that slashed up the middle on the mountain, you'll find the door half-way up on the right side. Trouble is you can't get up there."

"I don't see why not," Don protested, "I can climb like a goat. I'd fix a rope sling from the top of the mountain the way they go in the Alps, and I'd sit in it, and let Tim lower me down. Gee, I think that would be great, wouldn't it?"

"Then how would I get down?" demanded Tim. "Tie it to a bush and take a running high jump, I suppose. I do like the way you always manage to fix things for yourself, Don, and never think of me."

"I was thinking of you all the time. I didn't want you to get hurt," said Don.

" Precious, of course you never thought you'd get there first and take all the glory."

Sandy was calmly ignoring them both as he squatted on the ground and scanned the distant mountain through the telescope. " It's always been my idea," he said, " that someone, prospectors or Indians or maybe Spaniards, got tired travelling that seventy odd miles around the range, so they started to tunnel through right up that canyon. Maybe they just dug a big hole to store dynamite in when the mining boom was on, but I don't think so."

" I don't see how you ever could keep yourself from going up there and opening it right up once you'd found out about it and where it was? " Tim sat down on the top of the rock like the coyote, clasping her hands around her knees, and looking eagerly off at the mountain.

" Well, you see it was this way." Sandy waited until he had quite finished his gazing. Then he scratched his head with the small brass end of the telescope. " I figured it must have been put there for a purpose. Whoever made that door knew what he was doing, most likely he'd a right to put it there too. All right, now for the sake of argument, how do we know he won't come back some day if he is on this side of that door 'stid of the other side, and make trouble for anyone that's gone and bin foolish enough to disturb his calculations."

"But he may be on the inside of the door," said Tim thoughtfully.

"Then most surely I wouldn't dream of disturbing him, no, sirree." Sandy spoke firmly as he rose to leave. "I never knew any luck coming from visiting a skeleton in his last peaceful abode. Let 'em alone, says I. I've found skeletons of men out in the desert and up in the mountains and down in canyons, and I never so much as moved one of 'em one inch. Some day I hope I'll turn into a desert skeleton back there in my shack, and I'd like to be let alone. I can't think of any pleasanter way to stick around after you're dead than to just sit natural-like, tipped back in a chair against your own wall looking off at sunsets forevermore."

"Sandy, I do think you're a real poet," Tim exclaimed fervently. "Isn't that beautifully expressed, Don?"

"Well, I think he'd be an awful shock to tourists," said Don. "And Father says we ought to encourage them coming into the country and see what it's like."

Sandy did not seem to notice either of them. "Dave Watson came across the skeleton of a man propped up in bed in a lone cabin over in the Horseshoe once. And he told me he thought it was some homesteader or maybe an invalid that had strayed out to fade away in the sunshine. One day Dave got curious and climbed up to look in the window and what did he see but the skeleton natural as could be, propped up in bed with all his clothes on, reading a book."

"What was the book, Sandy?" Her eyes were wide with interest, and her voice a little bit awed.

"I didn't ask Dave that, you just mention it to him next time you see him. I know he reported it down to the sheriff's office, but nobody ever remembered anyone living up there, so Dave said he boarded up the shack and left him where he looked so mighty comfortable."

"Oh, Sandy," exclaimed Tim rapturously, "you do tell the most interesting, fascinating stories I ever heard in all my life. Just supposing that Don and I should find that shack some day and see him sitting there in bed. Wouldn't that be wonderful, Don?"

" Sure," said Don, " on a nice dark night when the coyotes are howling. I can just see you trying to get in, Tim. Anyway, it's all boarded up, isn't it, Sandy? "

" It sure is," Sandy agreed. " Now you two shove along toward home." They were down at the foot of the Splinter and had found the three ponies standing close together as if they had been enjoying a confab, Sandy said, all by themselves. All at once there came the hum of a motor far up overhead, and he whipped off his old gray felt hat and waved it back and forth. " See him? " he shouted. " See that boy sailing away up there? I watch for him every day when he goes over my place. That's the air mail and I've always wanted to meet that fellow. I've been on high seas and crossed plains and fought Indians and killed wild animals, but when it comes to real adventure, the boy that rides the clouds has got us all beat. I hang out a lantern on the side of the shack nights so in case one of 'em might be roaming around and lost his way, he'll get his bearings from that light. Run along now, and follow your noses. Good-bye."

They turned around to wave to him as they rode off, but Tim remained very silent and meditative until finally Don asked her what ailed her.

"Nothing. Just thinking. I believe I'll ask Father to let me hang out a lantern too at our place to let that air mail pilot know where he is. There isn't a landing field anywhere around, do you know that, Don, not at Frisbee, or even Oro. And lots of them fall."

"He doesn't go anywhere near our place," Don told her. "He has to cut right across the desert." Tim regarded him with a calm and measuring disdain.

"It's too bad," she said, "that I happen to be the only person in my whole family with any original ideas, and I notice that I have to carry them out myself, too. Anyway, just remember, I didn't ask you for any help, old pet."

"Help about what?"

"Nothing at all, only I know that Father will let me have all the land I want up back of the corral on the mesa for a landing field if I ask him for it."

"Who's going to fix it up? I suppose you think a landing field just grows that way?"

"It certainly does," Tim declared. "I saw one up at Williams once with Father when we were going to the canyon. As long as it's level enough and big enough, that's all that matters."

Don had pulled his pony up from a fast canter, and slipped out of the saddle to kneel and examine some tracks in the wagon road. A light wind had started to blow, and tumbleweed raced about like giant thistledown, leaving strange spidery tracks in the dust. "Look here," said Don. "Look at that track!"

"What of it? We rode by here when we came out." Tim did not even take the trouble to get down from her saddle but stood by on Chapo.

"See here." Don was tracing the hoof-prints with his hand. "They left the road here and started off straight for the mountains right by the Splinter, see that?" He showed her where the desert flowers had been crushed by passing hoofs. Tim jumped down to look also. "But there's only one horse," she said, "and they're fresh to-day. It couldn't have been Jim Quinn or the professor, Don."

"Who said it was?" Don sat back on his heels and grinned up at her. "Look at the way that left hind foot swings out and scuffs the ground. That's Pablo's pony. It caught its foot in a gopher hole and now when it's running it always hits out sideways with that hoof and scuffs."

"Do you think he's gone after them?"

"I don't know," Don said musingly. "If we had time, I'd ride back to the rock and see for sure if he circled around it and waited for the noon shadow to fall, and then hit out from that for the mountains. I tell you one thing that Sandy won't understand, and that is that someone else knows all about that shadow too, and that's Jim Quinn."

"You know what Sandy said about an Indian telling him about the shadow and the hidden lake and the gold and everything. Maybe Jim knows too, and maybe Pablo found out from him. That would be easy."

"I don't think Pablo knows anything, he's too stupid," said Don. "He's just curious like a fox, and he likes to hang around us boys and see what we're going to do next. Do you suppose he'd start off alone across the desert just out of curiosity? Wait till we get home and find out if he's gone some place."

"And see if he took supplies with him," agreed Tim. "You never did trust him, did you, Don?"

She was treating Don a little better now, and he took it graciously. "Well, I don't think he's vicious, but I just think he likes to nose around and find out about things. Dave Watson says he's all right, but even Dave's too easy-going ever to be suspicious of anyone."

Tim rode faster, and when she reached home the first thing she did was to run down to the kitchen after she had left Chapo in the corral. Certainly the pinto was gone, and when she asked Estrella where Pablo was, she smiled back at her peacefully.

"Hunt rabbit, take-a much-a eat," she said.

Don's eyes narrowed into a squint like Sandy's, and he chewed thoughtfully on the end of a pen holder. "I'm just writing a note to Sandy, and I'm going to leave it at Sam's for him. He'll come in Sunday morning sure to get things at the store, and I want to let him know about Pablo. And next week's Easter vacation so we've got plenty of time to do anything we want to."

"What do you think you'll do, Don?" Tim asked eagerly. "We ought to follow that trail."

"Did you just think of that? That's what I meant to do all along."

"But the wind will blow the tracks away."

"It can't straighten the crushed and trampled flowers, can it?"

She smiled at him with dawning understanding. "You know, Don, I do believe you've got real sense after all. Sometimes I just lose all hope when you act the way you do."

"What do you mean?" asked Don indignantly. "I act all right."

"Oh, I mean when you go away rabbit hunting with Neil or do something silly like that when there's real business to look after. Then all at once you get an idea and it cheers me all up. We'll start early Monday, won't we, and not say a word to anyone."

"If you do, I won't go, or else I'll get up before breakfast and go without you."

"I won't, truly," Tim promised, "not even Tom or Neil, only what will we do when we get to the Horseshoe? It will take most all day, won't it, and maybe we'll miss the right mountain, and supposing we don't see anything of Pablo when we do get there? Supposing you can't even find the place in the road where the hoof-prints were?"

"I'll find them," grinned Don. "I left two blue marbles right where they turned off to mark the place. Can't help but find them. I'd like to see any rabbit or gopher that could bolt a blue alley for dinner."

This time Tim just gazed at him in speechless admiration. "It's the strangest thing I ever saw," she said finally with a sigh, "it just proves you can't go by appearances at all. Here you look as if you didn't know anything special at all, Don, I mean you just look like any other boy, and Dick Thorpe's got a high forehead, and combs his hair straight back, and always looks as if he could speak on any subject at all, and he doesn't know anything. I wonder if we didn't have scout blood in our family, and it's come out in you. You're really wonderful."

Don took this unexpected praise sceptically. "And to-morrow you'll be saying I'm a dumb-bell and everything else. You think if a person isn't talking a blue streak all the time, and making wise cracks, they don't know anything. Just remember ' still waters don't splash.' "

" That isn't it at all," Tim corrected instantly. " It's ' Still waters run deep,' smarty."

" I like mine *better,*" retorted Don calmly.

CHAPTER VII

THE next morning Tim tried to get more definite information out of Estrella about why Pablo had gone away for a day or so and stayed away overnight when he had the horses to look after. Estrella smiled and shrugged her shoulders.

" He come back."

" But where did he go? " Tim persisted.

" Oro maybe, sell snakes."

" Can you imagine anything so silly? " Tim exclaimed when she told Don. " First she told me last night he'd gone to hunt rabbits, and to-day she says he's gone to Oro to sell snakes."

" What do you suppose he's doing? " asked Tom as he fixed a broken cinch strap.

" Oh, nothing, maybe just looking around for Jim Quinn and the old professor," Tim said.

" I heard over in town last night that the professor never hired Jim at all to guide him, he just took a notion into his head that there might be something doing and he trailed along to watch. Seems Jim was doing a little talking over at the store when he rode back after supplies. I'd laugh if the old man was really after what he said he was, just prehistoric remains and bones, and Jim got fooled thinking he was hunting for gold."

Don and Tim shot quick significant glances at each other. " Don't you think he went after gold in the first place, Tom? " asked Tim anxiously. " I mean the professor."

" I don't know. If he did, he's just another false alarm. Frisbee isn't on any gold or copper drift either. It's all conglomerate around here." Tom took his saddle on his shoulder and walked off toward the corral.

" He doesn't really know anything about it," Don said. " That's only his opinion, and he's an old stiff. Here comes Dave. Why don't you ask him? "

" I certainly will." Tim waved her hand to the ranger as he rode his big bay horse leisurely up the road to the mesa. " Good-morning, Mr. Watson, happy Easter! "

" Same to you, Tim." He stopped in front of the house and smiled down at the two. " Got here a little later than usual on account of a brush fire over on Lookout night before last. It kept me chasing for a couple of nights."

"Keeping it from spreading, you mean?" asked Don.

"Well, that and saving young birds. You see this time of the spring the grass and bushes are liable to have new nests and young birds in them, and when there's a fire, the old birds get pretty much frightened. I generally keep an eye on them. Couldn't do without the birds, you know. I often feel tempted to buy a parrot, I get so doggone lonesome way off yonder for a week at a time. I don't blame old Robinson Crusoe one bit for feeling he had to have something for company."

"My, Mr. Watson," said Tim fervently, "I wish I could be up there with you. I'd rather be a ranger than anything."

"I wouldn't, I'd rather be the captain of a ship that traded all over the world," Don put in.

"Oh, but then you just work for yourself, and if you're a ranger you're protecting everything. It's sort of—of heroic to be way off up there by yourself with all that wonderful responsibility."

Dave laughed and took off his big broad brimmed felt hat. "Well, I don't know, Tim, sometimes I don't just fancy glory altogether.

I'd like to take my mother and homestead some fine land."

"I know," Tim gazed up at him in deep admiration. "I'd like to do that too, but you look so handsome, Mr. Watson, in ranger clothes, I wouldn't change if I were you."

Dave fairly colored up to the roots of his curly close cut hair. "Ain't you ashamed to kid me like that on Easter morning, Tim?"

"Oh, but I wouldn't kid you for all the world," said Tim seriously. "Truly you do. Have you seen anything of Jim Quinn or the old man he went out with?"

"Seen their tracks and camp ashes. They're moving along trying to find a way through. After they've been in and out of every blind canyon from here to Azuba, they'll decide to get through by the main road same as everybody."

"Or maybe you'll come across their skeletons some day," Tim said very soberly. Dave chuckled as he swung off his horse.

"You're sure wishing them luck, Tim," he replied, as he went into the house to see Mr. McLean.

"Did you ask him if he'd seen Pablo?" asked

Don the first thing. "Or tell him about the tracks we found?"

"I certainly did not," answered Tim with dignity; "do you think I'm giving away all our secrets? I never mentioned Pablo's name. Rangers never really notice anything except what they are expected to look after, and that's fires. I wouldn't bother asking him anything about Pablo when his mind was all taken up with a fire even if it was only a little one."

"I think you might have asked him if he'd seen Pablo," Don persisted.

"Listen to me, Donald Scott McLean," Tim stood before him in fighting position, her tousled head down like a young rooster, "if you think I'm going to tell everybody what I think before I've got any real proof, you're mistaken. We're only suspicious of Pablo because he acts so queer and because we know he's ridden off toward the Horseshoe and that one special mountain."

"Gee, Tim, you just make up your mind to one thing and then go and turn everything upside down. Didn't you say that Pablo was after Jim and didn't you think maybe Jim had got him to run away from here and join him?"

"Well, I do believe all that," Tim agreed. "But I can't prove it, can I? I don't care what Tom says, I think they're all after the same thing. You know that lump of gold Sandy showed us. There's some place where it came from, and the professor thinks he knows where it is, and Jim's following him to find out, and I think that Pablo's trailing after both of them. Maybe because he's part Mexican, he doesn't want anybody to find out where gold is. Now that is perfectly logical, Don." Tim's eyes were round and serious. "You heard Sandy yourself when he said there was gold in a secret place in the mountains and the Indians knew and wouldn't tell. I never heard anything that sounded so true as his story about that Indian he helped."

"Applesauce," answered Don. "You can swallow anything, Tim. Why don't you think for yourself like I do?"

"All right, then, what do you think?"

"I'm going to keep it to myself. When you get a secret you're never satisfied until you've tried it out on Dave or something to see what they think about it."

"I never told Dave Watson a thing, Don, and

I think you're mean even to suppose that I would do such a thing." Tim turned around indignantly and walked into the house to get dressed for church. It was time anyway, but she wanted to make a dignified and impressive exit before Don. He never even looked up after her, though, just went on reading his comic section as usual. Why did boys have to be so aggravating, she thought, but maybe they couldn't help it. It was just their nature to always go opposite from the way you expected them to go. The more she thought over this while she was dressing, the surer she felt that Don wanted to go by himself without her all the time. He was trying his best to discourage her and make her think there wasn't anything strange about Pablo's leaving the ranch without permission.

Easter service was so impressive and beautiful that she forgot all about Don until she came out of church and looked about for him and Neil to go home with her. Instead she noticed Dick Thorpe looking across at her. She knew he was looking at her and yet it was almost as if he were looking right through her, because he didn't show any sign of recognition at all, and he was frowning a little too. It ruffled Tim immediately, and she sauntered directly over past him and made believe she never saw him.

" Hello," said Dick, quite informally for him, " when are you going riding in the desert? "

" Why, to-morrow." It flashed instantly across Tim's active mind that here was a good way to get even with Don and make him sorry he'd been so snooty with her over his old secret. Not that she would tell the Thorpes, of course, but they might ride out as far as the Splinter with her, and maybe a little farther. " We'll have to start early, though. Do you think you could be at the ranch by eight or half past? Will Margot go too? Do you want to use our horses? "

They walked out of the little stone church together and Tim saw Don give them a quick inquiring glance when he came out from the choir room. She turned carelessly and smiled at Dick.

" Yes, two of them. My father can't come, but we'll be there at eight."

" Do you ride western? "

" Certainly." He regarded her with his clear, unsmiling blue eyes, and Tim was instantly seized with a savage longing to see him perched up on

Tom's Buckskin and let Buck really start to do his stuff. She might let Margot have Chapo, and she could take Quien Sabe, Neil's easy-going bronco. And wouldn't Don have a little thrill of surprise when he knew what she had done? It would serve him right for teasing her.

" How's the car going now? " she asked, very innocently, and Dick became more distant than ever.

" Very well, thanks."

" Oh, not at all. Do you know how to shoot? "

" Of course." But this time she knew she had aroused his interest. " Why? "

" I thought maybe you'd like to go out hunting with the boys some day. Quail or rabbit."

" You don't have any big game here, do you? "

" Nothing but mountain lion. I shot one up in the High Sierras when we were camping there last year, and I've got the pelt."

" How did you learn to shoot? "

" Hitting corks out of bottles without breaking the glass. I can do it at thirty feet."

Margot had seen them and was waving to her and trying to make Dick understand he must come along to the car.

"Suppose we bring some bottles with us to-morrow," he said in a friendlier way. "I'll have my own gun. How about lunch?"

"I'll tell Estrella to fix us a lot of chicken tamales and fruit and all sorts of things. We can eat when we get to the Splinter."

"You can't carry a lunch on horseback."

"How do you suppose we ever eat then when we're riding a long way? You have to carry a pack back of the saddle, goose."

Dick looked as if he wanted to warn her not to call him goose, but as it was, he nodded quickly and went after Margot. What would he say, she wondered, when he found out that Don was not going with them? Almost she made up her mind on the way home to speak to Don and be friends, but he never even noticed her, and all that afternoon he and the other boys were down working on the cars. Tim never could see why boys loved to fuss around cars and try to take them to pieces and put them together again on a hot day and get just as dirty and greasy as they possibly could.

But after supper that night when she was out on the porch all alone in the couch hammock and feeling as blue as could be and deserted, Don came strolling up.

" We'll start off about seven," he said casually.

" I've made all my own plans, thanks," Tim replied haughtily. " And I can keep them a secret too."

" All right, I'll go by myself then, only don't say I didn't invite you to come along."

" I don't have to get any special invitation from you to ride out on the whole desert, do I?"

" Nice, sweet little kitty cat," teased Don. " I suppose you're going to take those Thorpes along with you and tell them all about it. Why don't you invite the whole town?"

" We're only going for a ride."

" Well, I hope Dick Thorpe enjoys a whole day with just you two girls. He'll have a fine time."

Tim was annoyed and bothered because she was doubtful about Dick's enjoyment herself when he found out that Don was not to be one of the party. " You're not going way off by yourself to the mountains anyway," she said. " I don't see why you don't either go with us, or wait for us at the Splinter. He wants to shoot at corks and rabbits and gophers and things."

" Tell him for me to see if he can hit the Splinter," laughed Don, and he dodged the magazine she hurled at his head. It hit Estrella instead, but she stood in the doorway with her broad, kindly smile, holding a warm Indian blanket.

"Too cold," she said, and wrapped it all around Tim as she threw herself back in the hammock, and the loving patting and petting almost brought Tim to the verge of lonely tears.

" Oh, dear! Estrella, I wish Mother'd come home," she said. " She won't be here now until the middle of May. And I can't bear boys much longer. They're terrible. Where's Pablo really and truly, tell me, please, Estrella, like an old darling."

Estrella made her black eyes round like moons and very mysterious. " Much-a much-a snake before fire come too soon," she said. She slipped away noiselessly in her flat woven sandals, and left Tim sitting bolt upright staring after her.

CHAPTER VIII

As she rode out through the canyon toward the desert the next morning with the Thorpes Tim thought they would surely find Don lingering along the way somewhere waiting for them to catch up. Estrella told her when she got up that Don had been in for his breakfast even before his father and Tom, and had gone away on Dusty around seven.

Dick asked her where her brother was and Tim felt provoked and embarrassed too at Don acting like this when he knew they were coming to the ranch. It was all very well scrapping and skirmishing in the bosom of one's own family, in fact it was fun sometimes and made things more interesting, but when it came to showing off before strangers, Tim frankly did not like it. It wasn't comradely or loyal even, she decided, not that Dick and Margot didn't have their own troubles together, but at least they were well bred about it, and never showed off before people.

Altogether the farther away from the ranch they rode, the more indignant Tim became at

Don for his independence and uppishness with her. He knew perfectly well that she was going to ride out to the Splinter whether he went with her or not, but come to think of it, she had not told Don the Thorpes were going with her. But she knew too that Don would never have approved of her taking them to the Splinter, or showing them any of the McLeans' particular desert secrets. As they rode along Tim grew more and more anxious to see Don's head suddenly pop out at them. She simply must not take them over to the rock or anywhere along the trail to the door in the mountain. Then an idea came to her. Of course, how simple, she would take them up to Dave Watson's ranger cabin on Lookout, and they'd have a wonderful adventure. As soon as she thought of it, Tim felt all better and relaxed.

"I brought a bottle along with a cork in it," Dick told her. "I want to see you shoot the cork out of the bottle without breaking the glass the way you said you could."

"I'll shoot six corks if you like. Why didn't you bring a couple of bottles along so you could try too?"

" Because I'd only carry one for him," Margot said. " He stuck the bottle in my coat pocket because he wasn't wearing any."

" Give it to me and I'll stick it down in my saddle pocket." Tim reached over and took the bottle from Margot and put it safely down behind her in the deep pocket of her western saddle.

" I never saw a saddle like that before," Dick remarked, riding nearer to look at Tim's. It was a heavily embossed Mexican saddle of deep russet leather, highly polished, and studded with many little silver heads like tacks. On each side was a deep pocket, with a heavy strapped flap over it.

" They're really for extra pistols in the old days," Tim explained. " This saddle and horse belong to my big brother, Tom, and he got them down in Mexico. They belonged to a bandit and Tom wouldn't take any price for them, he's so proud of owning them. Buckskin is a very wonderful horse and can do all sorts of tricks. I was going to let you ride him this morning, Dick, but I was afraid he'd get notional with you."

" I can ride any horse," Dick announced curtly.

"Oh, Dick, stop showing off," Margot laughed. "Don't notice him at all, Tim."

"I don't mind if he wants to," Tim answered. She pulled Buckskin up short, and slipped off him. Buckskin stood still, switching his long tail slightly from side to side, and looking gentle and tame. Dick left Quien Sabe and came over to mount, but the very instant his foot touched the wooden stirrup, Buckskin wheeled about like lightning, and stood up on his hind legs pawing the air, then quite as suddenly, dropped down as if he was going to kneel and say his prayers. On second thought though, he doubled up like a jackknife and jumped straight up in the air. Don shot off over his head and landed several yards away on the ground. And Buckskin promptly subsided and turned into a quiet, mild looking horse.

"Are you all right?" called Tim cheerfully, but Dick did not answer, not even when Margot called to him to quit and ride Quien Sabe. He got up from his fall, his blonde hair rumpled over his blazing eyes, his jaws set, and even before Buckskin knew his intention, he was in the saddle again. This time he knew what was coming and

was not taken by surprise, and when Buckskin
tried his tricks again, Dick was ready for him.
After a few futile efforts to throw him off, buck-
ing and trying to roll, Buckskin bolted straight
ahead, ears laid back flat and the whites of his
eyes showing.

Tim stood up in her saddle to watch them go,
the first admiration she had ever felt for Dick
showing in her excited face and eyes.

" Look at him ride," she cried. " Margot,
look! "

" Oh, Dick can ride if he wants to," Margot
said carelessly. " That horse certainly can buck,
though. I couldn't have stayed on him one second. How can you ride him, Tim? It looks impossible now."

" I don't know, I guess he just lets me," said
Tim. " Look, he's slowing down."

Buckskin came trotting back tossing his head
and looking sheepish, and Dick had a queer little
grin on his face. " I like him," he said. " I wish
your brother'd sell him to me, but of course he'd
never do that. He's a bully horse. How old is
Tom? "

" Nineteen." Tim couldn't help showing that

she approved of his nerve and horsemanship. " You managed Buck splendidly."

" Oh, he's all right," Dick said briefly. " How many brothers have you got? "

" Three. Neil's the youngest, twelve. He's training water puppies to-day."

" Training what? " Margot asked eagerly.

" Water puppies, little funny lizards that you find in streams way up back in the canyon. They've got the queerest heads that look exactly like very young puppies and little tiny paws. Neil found five yesterday and he's keeping two for himself and taking the rest to school for nature study. He named his Fido and Rover. I'll show them to you when we get back. Maybe you'd like to take one home with you."

" I'd love to hide one in Tumpy's bed, wouldn't you, Dick? " said Margot.

" She's so stupid, she'd roll on it. I think I'd like one myself. Can you really train them? "

" Well, of course they don't bark," Tim told him teasingly, " but you might teach them to stand up and beg and catch things. Neil is teaching them to walk around a hoop. He takes a big barrel hoop and starts them walking around on it, one behind the other single file, and they do look so comical following after each other so earnestly while he turns the hoop around slowly."

" Where can I find some? "

" Up in the canyon above our mesa. I'll take you there or you can go with the boys. You have to wade way into the pools where the brook is deep, and you'll find them around the rocks. They don't try to run away from you, and of course, they never bite. Want to go with the boys next time? "

" Yes, I'd like to." Margot looked at Dick curiously. She had never seen him like this before, wanting to go out in the wilds like any other boy and rough it.

" Mother'll be back home in May, and then we'll have a lot of good times because she always thinks up things to do that are interesting."

" I never knew you had a mother alive! " exclaimed Margot. She gave Tim a quick, startled glance. " Where is she? "

" Visiting my grandmother and aunts back in Buffalo. What made you think that? "

" I don't know, seeing you alone the first day with that Mexican woman, perhaps. I liked you then, or at least, I felt as if I wanted to know you. We haven't any mother. She died in Africa when Dick and I were very young."

Dick rode on ahead, silent and with an odd expression on his face, as if he didn't care to hear any more about mothers. Tim hardly knew what to say. Margot spoke very naturally without any emotion, and yet Tim felt somehow behind her manner and words there must be something strange and sad. She gave her a quick look of sympathy.

" It must be awfully hard not to have a mother."

" We were both very little, Dick was only three and I was five. We had a native nurse, and were living way in the interior at a sort of big farm, the way they have them there. Father had gone away on an expedition for the government, and we were to join him later at Nairobi. I had a little pet deer that one of the native boys had caught and tamed for me, one of the dwarf antelope species, I forget what they are called, and I was playing with him over near the goat corral. I can just remember something that sprang over my head and then the shouts of the

women and men as a lioness seized the deer.
And I ran to try and save it. It was crouched
over the body of the deer, and when it saw me,
I think it was about to leap on me when my
mother pushed me aside and levelled a gun at it.
She shot it in the shoulder, but it sprang at her
and she fell. Before the boys could rush up and
kill the animal, she was dead. That's why my
father always has Dick and myself travel with
him. He never wants to be away from us."

"Oh," breathed Tim in horror, "oh, and just
think, I really and truly wanted Dick to ride
Buckskin to teach him a lesson, and he might
easily have been killed."

"Oh, that's all right," said Margot. "He en-
joyed it."

"But—but, that's the saddest story I ever
heard. No wonder you two just stick together.
I shot a mountain lion once all by myself when
we were camping out in the High Sierras, but I
didn't even know what it was until it toppled
down. Don and I were together and it was at
night. We had to go some distance from the
tents after water, and it was our turn to keep
the buckets filled, and we had forgotten, so we

took them and started off together, and Don told
me to go back after my gun because there might
be something around. And while he was dipping
up the water, I heard a creaking overhead and
saw two eyes like balls of fire on a bough right
over him. I thought it was a wildcat, and I shot
at it right between the eyes. And it crashed
down on the ground, and thrashed about a minute
and lay still. We ran and told Father, and I've
got the pelt in my room at home. But a real
African lion ——"

"Let's not talk about it, please," said Margot.
They rode along the old wagon road that led
from the mesa, where the ranch stood, up over
the Ridge where Pablo had said he saw the last
of Jim Quinn and the professor. From here
they could look out over the desert and Tim
found she had struck another novelty that interested Dick when she showed him the fossils of
strange reptile-like shapes embedded in the rock,
and many shells that seemed to have been welded
together into a curious pattern in the stone
formation.

"I'm sure that must have been a periwinkle,"
Margot declared as they stopped to examine one

place in the rock. She pointed out a perfect periwinkle shape and another one that was an unbroken scallop shell. "The sea must have been all through here some time. Remember, Dick, when we stopped at Torrey Pines for luncheon, we saw the same thing, and that was way up in the air on a mountain top. There must have been part of the ocean all over this long ago."

When they had ridden on over the Ridge they came to the end of the down trail and Tim said to let the ponies have a good run after their hard climb down, it would get all the nonsense out of them. Buckskin galloped after the other two, but his enthusiasm seemed to have quieted down a little, and Chapo came out ahead. Tim had taken the opposite direction from the Splinter on purpose and they were headed west now toward Lookout Mountain where Dave Watson had his cabin.

"That looks like smoke over yonder," Dick said, pointing to a wing-like shadow far off over Lookout. It did not seem to stir but hung heavily in the bright blue sky. Margot was only interested in the Judas trees, and had to ride up close to one and pick some of its strange white blossoms. As far as they could see riding this way, the cacti and Judas trees seemed to own the desert. They rose here and there like strange surprised animals resenting any trespassing.

"You can use their spikes for paper cutters," Tim said. "I don't like the flowers because they're oozy. The cactus flower is very sweet and they say the Indians used to gather the heart and make candy out of it. When a young brave fell in love, and wanted to prove how brave he was, he would go out at night and attack a big cactus, and cut away its sharp thorns and leaves until he reached the heart. Then he had to cut that all down to the sweet core and that had to be cooked and cooked in a certain way until all the syrup was out of it, and then made that into candy. It makes them seem more human, doesn't it, to think they ever liked candy? You can buy cactus candy now down in Frisbee and Oro. I guess it's about the same."

"We'll get some next time we go to Sam's," Margot said. "Only of course it wouldn't have the real romance about it now. That is smoke, isn't it?"

"Yes, but it's just a little brush fire." Tim glanced back over her shoulder, and saw someone riding behind them at a gallop. At first she thought it was Don, and her heart beat faster, to think he was coming to join them, after all, but instead it turned out to be Dave Watson. She waved to him, and he slowed up when he caught up to them.

"That fire's broke out again," he said. "They called me up on the 'phone from Oro, but I was working all night with some other fellows and we had it under control this morning. I just rode twelve miles down to the electric light plant at the dam to get word to Frisbee for help. The telephone poles burned and the lines are down. You had better turn around for home."

"Oh, Mr. Watson, I want to go with you and see the fire," protested Tim eagerly. "Honestly we won't be a bit of trouble, we can help you, because we can ride and take messages for you and everything. Please, Mr. Watson."

"Well, all right, come along. There's nobody at my cabin. You can go up there and make coffee if you want to, and get some food together for the men out on the fire-lines."

"We'd love to do that," exclaimed Tim. "I forgot to introduce you to my friends, Margot and Dick Thorpe."

"How are you?" called Dave cordially, as he galloped away, and waved back to them.

"Who is he?" asked Dick.

"One of my very best friends," said Tim fervently. "I think I'd trust Dave Watson next to my own father. He just simply knows everything about this country."

"What is his work like?"

"He's a ranger," Tim's tone was ringing with pride as she said it. "If I were a man I'd rather be a ranger than anything."

"He rode like a cavalryman, didn't he, Dick?"

"Oh, he's been in the army," Tim cried. "He's seen service in the Islands and he was in the World War. I'll tell you all about him some time. Come on, now." She gave her pony full rein, and Quien Sabe was off like a rocket with the other two following fast. Over Lookout the strange saffron-colored cloud was slowly billowing out now, larger and larger. Even while she rode toward it, Tim was wondering where Don was, and sorry he was going to miss it.

CHAPTER IX

WITH the cloud of smoke rising about Lookout Mountain to guide them, Tim said she was sure she could find her way easily up to Mr. Watson's cabin. She had been there with Don and with her father, and she knew there was a short cut over a trail this side the mountain instead of being obliged to travel way around to the main motor highway.

After they had ridden for a long while and found only the rugged, barren washes and arroyos slashing in the range here and there, Tim drew up Chapo to really get her bearings.

" The trouble is that every last one of these mountains for thirty miles looks just like all the others when you're some distance from them, but there's the smoke," she pointed over beyond the amethyst-colored mountains, " so it must be the other side of Lookout where the fire's broken out."

Don pointed out what seemed to be a well-defined trail leading into a canyon ahead of them. "That seems to have been used a good deal," he said. "Why not try it?"

Tim agreed, but added with a sigh that was half angry, if only Don was with them, he knew every foot of the way.

"Where do you suppose he went? I thought he'd be with us to-day," Margot said. "That was one reason why Dick wanted the trip. He doesn't know any worth-while boys out here."

"You never can tell where Don may turn up." Tim tried to turn the matter off carelessly. "He started off by himself early, but I had an idea he'd be out in the desert waiting for us."

"It's rather a large place to find anyone in."

"Oh, well, we always make for either the Splinter or Sandy's. We'd better hurry because it's four or five miles up to the cabin and by the time we get there, the fire may be all out."

Tim tried to make believe she was not at all concerned over Don as she rode ahead, but she felt tired and bothered the more she wondered what had become of him. Perhaps he had ridden over to Sandy's by himself, and then again, it was more likely that he had started off to find the way from the Splinter to the door in the moun-

tain without her. If he had, Tim thought
fiercely, she'd never forgive him, never. It was
all very well to get a little angry and act up,
but there were certain things you just didn't do
to each other if you held to the code of fair play
and comradeship. If Don had chosen to chase
way off by himself after the secret of the door
when it was all her idea first, then she almost
hoped that something would happen to him to
punish him good and plenty. Tim was very
superstitious about playing fair. If one did not,
she firmly believed that something would surely
happen to one unexpectedly. Don would probably say that she herself had not been fair to him
asking the Thorpes to go riding the same day,
but how about him getting so fussy and on his
dignity with her, and saying very well, then, he'd
go by himself without her?

According to Tim's idea of family warfare you
went just so far, but you never really did anything spiteful or revengeful, and certainly Don
had been final with her. He needn't have been
so positive and cross about it as if she could never
go to the door in the mountain herself. He
could have been pleasant and ridden out with the

Thorpes just as well as not. Margot glanced
at her with amused curiosity. "What are you
scolding to yourself about? You're mumbling
away and nodding your head, what is it?"

"Oh, nothing," Tim tossed her head for a
change airily. "I was just thinking about something. I'm sure this is the right road because
there's the place where you cross the creek to the
other side."

They had travelled along the narrow trail for
some time until it dipped to a low ford and the
ponies picked their way through the rushing shal-
low water that wound its way over the round
bleached rocks and the gaunt old boughs of dead
trees that had fallen down into the creek years
ago. Here and there as they rode up the trail
again, a lone cottonwood gave a patch of shade,
but it was still and hot in the canyon the farther
up they went, and the flowers looked dusty and
drooping. The trail became so crumbly and
steep that the ponies hesitated, picking their way
as cautiously as cats along a fence rail. Tim
assured them it would get better the higher they
went. "You see it has been travelled often,
probably when Mr. Watson rides over it twice a

week. He has to go everywhere through the
mountains. It's awfully pretty way up here,
don't you think so?"

Margot agreed, but Dick did not answer. He
was keeping one eye on the trail and the other
on a cloud of smoke that seemed to rise slowly
beyond the next mountain and mushroom out like
a waterspout. It was much larger than when
they had seen it from the desert, and he wondered
whether they were riding straight into the fire
zone, or if they might not come out on top of the
mountain above where the fire seemed to be. He
asked Tim and she said they would find the
rangers' cabin right up on top of Lookout, and
she was positive it was the next mountain to their
left. But the country grew wilder and more
desolate and they were so high that they could
look down on the lower ranges that dipped in
great waves to meet the desert. The sagebrush
cast a soft purplish haze over the land and cacti
reared up here and there like some strange kind
of startled animals. The gophers scampered
across the trail under the ponies' hoofs as they
dashed for their holes, and then on second
thought, sat up to take a good look at the in-

truders.   Tim showed them a gopher snake moving softly along the ground behind some rocks,
and said they were the only enemy a gopher was
really afraid of.   Young rabbits too, hopped
frantically out of their way, comical little half
grown Molly Cottontails.   Dick wished they had
time to stop and get a potshot at them, but Tim
said they must keep on going because she was
going to make coffee for Dave Watson and his
fire fighters.

" I'll bet you never get there," Dick called out
to her, but just then the trail came out on top
of the mountain and there was the cabin just as
she had said it would be, right on top of Lookout.
" The fire's burning just as I said it was, over
in the west canyon, and the wind's blowing south-
east."

. " And if it shifts about the fire will climb
Lookout."

" Oh, it won't," Tim declared happily, as she
let Chapo take his own pace now.   When they
reached the next resting place they could see
where the fire lay.   It had evidently broken out
on the canyon side west of Lookout and was
burning heavily.   From where they watched it,

they could see the smoke welling out in great
slowly spreading spirals from the dry brush and
grass, with only a deep sulphurous glow underneath to show how fiercely it was blazing. Margot wondered how it could have started.

"Campers or motor tourists," Tim told her.
"They toss a half burned cigarette out and never
think how it will smoulder and set fire to the
dry grass. We'll hit the main road now very
soon."

"Oh, but I thought the cabin would be Mexican rose stucco, or something like that," Margot
exclaimed disappointedly. "That's only built of
logs, isn't it?"

"Slabs, I think," Tim smiled over at her
teasingly, and couldn't help but notice how pretty
Margot looked in her riding outfit, white linen
breeches, trim white riding shirt, and sleeveless
coat of green broadcloth with real tan riding
boots. Tim felt a little conscious for the first
time of her own rough and ready appearance,
but as a matter of fact, she liked it. It was very
comfortable and her usual riding costume, old
corduroy breeches, Neil's belt, and an old pongee
shirt open wide at the throat with a red silk

Mexican scarf knotted around it that she was very fond of. She did not realize what a picturesque figure she made on Chapo, with her thick brown hair curling to her shoulders, her tanned eager face, and wide interested gray eyes. As she rode ahead she was thinking what a sight she would be riding with the Thorpes in a big city.

The cabin seemed to fade away the nearer they got to it as the smoke swept low down around the top of the mountain and hid it from sight. They reached it finally, and Tim led the way inside. It was very plainly furnished, a couple of army cots and two wooden tables, a small rusty iron stove and a cupboard. Joe Wyler sat at one of the tables with earphones clamped to his head, busy as a jaybird, but he glanced up and nodded, and Tim went over to him and leaned down to call in one ear:

"Mr. Watson told me to come up and make some coffee." She pointed to Dick and Margot. "This is Dick and Margot Thorpe, friends of mine, Joe."

Joe took a good look at Dick. "You can get on your horse and ride to the ridge. Tell any of

the men over there that the fire's broken out
above the crossing and the bridge's burned. Get
hold of Dave if you can."

He gave the order in a tone that gave no
chance for any argument, but Dick took it eagerly and turned about to go for Buckskin.
Tim really felt proud of him the way he obeyed
orders like that, but Margot said he'd been a
Boy Scout in England, and of course he knew
just what to do in emergencies.

"Well, I think I'll turn my brothers into
scouts too, then," Tim announced. "They'd
stand and argue by the hour." They went to the
corner of the cabin that appeared to be the
kitchen domain and Tim raided the woodpile for
kindling and firewood while Margot hunted for
the waterpail. There was a regular mountain
boarding house coffee pot on a shelf behind the
cupboard, high and large all around without any
percolator fancy trimmings. The coffee certainly gave out a delicious aroma when it started
to boil and Joe motioned to them to bring him
some. He drank it thirstily and told them to
make plenty, as he went back to his listening
station.

Tim hunted about until she located a big tin of crackers and some condensed milk and sugar, and finally a lot of canned baked beans. " Now, they'll have plenty to eat as they come in," she said with satisfaction as she turned the beans out in a deep pan and popped them into the oven.

Margot was interested in listening to Joe as he answered calls on the wire. Motorists were being held up on the ridge route, and made to either stay and fight or turn back. The fire was sweeping over the creek, but under control along the ridge. Every boy or man in the region had been sent for to help. When Tim handed him his second cup of coffee, Joe motioned to her to take the glasses from their case on the wall and go out and look at the fire.

From where they stood on top of Lookout, it was almost like being in an airplane looking down at the panorama of canyon and mesa between the two mountains. The smoke rose in a monstrous wind-blown wing now and showed where the flames were advancing through the new area, leaving behind huge blackened spaces and smouldering tree trunks.

A car came puffing up the road with two boys

in it, and Tim recognized them as friends of Tom's, Slim and Custer Bryan. Stuck in helter-skelter around the rear of their old car were shovels, pails, hoes, and old clothes turned into big mops. "To beat out the fire in the grass," Tim told Margot. "Hello, Slim, how's the fire? Want some hot coffee and beans?"

The two boys grinned at her, smoke grimed and perspiring. "Do we? Say, we've been hitting the brush since early this morning, ever since Don gave the alarm from the electric light plant."

"Did Don do that?" Tim exclaimed. "The idea! Isn't he wonderful? I mean he just thinks he's wonderful, that's all."

"Well, he sent the first alarm to Joe here and got hold of Dave." They went on into the cabin, and Tim looked at Margot with a funny little smile.

"Did you hear what he said? Don gave the first alarm. Probably that was why he couldn't ride with us." All at once she felt amazingly proud of Don and forgot all about how angry she had been with him. "It's just like him to do that, he's like Father," she said. "I wish we could ride over and take coffee to Mr. Watson and the others who are fighting fire. They'll never have time to come up here. Come on, let's, Margot."

There was no time to consider further as the two boys came hurrying out of the cabin and had to get back at once, so Tim took the big coffee pot under her special guardianship, and piled cups, sugar and condensed milk into a basket for Margot to carry, then they climbed to the rear seat of the old roadster.

"Why didn't we ride down on the ponies?" Margot said as they bumped and swayed over the rocky mountain road under Slim's hasty and imperative driving.

"Not with this pot of hot coffee. Do you think I could ever balance it on Chapo? Besides, horses are terribly afraid of fire and they're no good anywhere around if they smell smoke, are they, boys? They just get frightened and bolt." Tim held the pot on an even base firmly, but still it splashed a little, and she was relieved when they finally drew up alongside the lower bend of the road and the boys told them just where they could cut through and reach the men.

Tim climbed down first and Margot handed the coffee pot after her. There was an empty pail left in the car, and she set the pot in that and bolstered it up with twigs and leaves so it could not dance around. It was ever so much easier to carry this way, and would keep hot longer, she thought, so they followed Custer into the deep brush while Slim took the other direction to the new danger spot where the fire had jumped the creek and was burning up the opposite side of the canyon.

" Aren't these stickers terrible? " Margot said as she scrambled through the tall dry grass and briers. " I'm glad we have boots on."

" Don't think about anything except getting there! " Tim called back, as she plunged ahead trying to keep Custer in sight. Finally he got so far ahead of them that even his blue shirt was lost to sight, and they had to depend on listening to the smashing and crackling as he pushed through the heavy brush.

They were heading straight into the fire zone now with the smoke billowing up ahead of them until it seemed as if it mushroomed out against the blue sky like a water spout. There was hardly any wind, except an occasional light breeze from the south that sent the smoke wavering like a filling sail. A mountain brook still swollen from the spring rains had spread out over one small arroyo they had to pass, but they had to go through or be left behind. Remembering Margot's new riding boots, Tim called back to her encouragingly, "They'll dry!"

"I wish we'd find Dick," said Margot. "Is he over here?"

"I don't know." Tim was scrambling breathlessly up a long steep stretch of wash that was mostly dry rocks but at the end she caught sight of Custer's blue shirt in the distance and the first line of fire fighters. They were scattered so far apart that the girls set up their coffee stand on a fallen log and served as the men came up. It was very exciting with the fire burning right over the first dip of land from where they stood. Tim said she felt as if she was right up to the first line trenches in the war zone, and as if she had crossed No Man's Land with the coffee pot.

"It was lots of fun, though," Margot exclaimed as they started off to find the next line-up on Lookout. "Didn't they enjoy it?"

"Did I? Only all the time I was wishing I'd run across Don."

"And I was wishing we'd find Dick so we could give him some."

"You're just as much a goose over him as I am over Don, you worry over him all the time. Haven't you found out they never bother about us, they just go on their own way rejoicing and never even think what we're doing."

The way grew dangerously steep and rough and Tim had to curb her conversation much against her inclination, in order to safely convey the coffee pot. She held it high over her head as she tried to push her way through a wall of thorny mesquite and brush, and finally emerged breathless and hot on the other side. "Did you ever play that game about, 'When do you coffee pot, where do you coffee pot?'" she called back merrily. "I could act it all out this minute."

But Margot was staring away from her off at the cloud of smoke. "Isn't the wind changing?" she asked. "That smoke seems to be blowing this way!"

CHAPTER X

TIM stood still and stared too at the cloud of smoke, dove colored now overhead, and shutting out the sunlight. "It doesn't look very good, does it? I wish we were up to Mr. Watson and his men. Maybe Dick's there too by now."

"No, Joe said he was to patrol the main road and stop motorists. I guess we have plenty of time to climb higher and get through. Is this the way to the ridge trail?"

"I should say it isn't. The ridge trail is way off, over beyond the wash, and then up as high as you can go on that side of the canyon. We're headed for the place where the boys said Mr. Watson was. Wait a minute." She sent out a long whistling call, and there came an answer to their left. Presently a couple of hails came again, much nearer this time, and a man showed up out of the brush in the distance.

"Hello, Barty," shouted Tim. "Is it safe to go through to Mr. Watson this way?"

"Safe as any," responded Barty laconically as he wiped off his face with the back of his hand

and leaned on his shovel. "It's getting hotter every minute through the canyon here. Why don't you girls turn back?"

"Can't. We're carrying coffee." Tim felt very proud as she said this. "Have some?"

"Don't mind if I do." Barty reached them after a minute or so, scrambling through the brush, and drank a cup of coffee down gratefully. "That certainly goes to the right spot," he said. "Mighty fine of you to bring it to us. Thanks. I have to get back."

"There's a trail up through this side of the canyon, isn't there, Barty?"

"There is, but I'd advise you to go on back. Fire's playing new tricks on us every minute, and I heard from Slim it had jumped the creek and was working up Lookout now. Dave's got a fellow on horseback on the main road corralling every one that comes along and telling them to either get out and fight fire or get on back where they come from."

Margot leaned forward with shining eyes. "That's my brother, Dick Thorpe. He's on Buckskin."

Barty looked at her keenly over the rim of his

second cup. "Are you two Chandler's young-sters?" he asked. "Mining engineer down in Frisbee? I'll bet a dollar he don't know you two kids are up fighting fire!"

"He wouldn't mind." Margot gave him a handful of crackers and cheese, and he went back into the brush. She looked after him with a puz-zled expression. "They don't like Father out here, do they?"

"They never like any newcomers, especially from the east," Tim replied. "It's just their way. Barty Green's a regular old mountain gopher anyway, dug himself a house out of the side of the canyon and stuck an army cot up there, and never works if he can help it. I'll bet a cookie he got smoked out, that's why he's work-ing. I didn't give him any milk or sugar in that last cup. And I don't believe what he says about that trail. There is a good one right down lower from here, and we can strike it if we try."

"But the smoke is getting worse. Don't you think we'd better stay on the higher level?"

"It's much shorter the other way." Tim was surprised to find Margot questioning her author-ity in wilderness matters. "I'm going."

through the land and trailing long garments of flame with its face veiled in smoke. Frightened birds flew wildly before it clamoring and calling to their young, and the girls saw a bevy of young quail fluttering to safety up the side of the rocks where they themselves were.

"It's coming now," Margot said. "Take a deep, deep breath, and cover up your head."

She put her arms around Tim, and Tim clasped her tightly. She had always wanted a big sister, and Margot was like one now in her protective way and coolness. Like an enormous tidal wave the fire broke through the canyon where they had been. It seemed to flow widely across it, covering everything in its path. The girls closed their eyes and buried their faces in their hands. For a moment it seemed as if they could not possibly draw another breath in the stifling hot blast and choking smoke that swept over them, and then it had passed by. When they opened their eyes and looked with smarting, blinking lids about them, it seemed as if the whole lower canyon had been scorched and blackened as if blasted by lightning.

"That was a close call," said Tim, solemnly.

" Margot, you were simply wonderful. I'm terribly sorry for what I said, and you were right. Here I've been thinking that I ——"

" Oh, please don't," Margot laughed. " You make me feel awfully silly. Which way is the ridge trail from here? I'm all turned about and confused."

Tim pointed to the first long ridge above them in the canyon. " If we just keep on climbing, we'll come out there, and we're sure to get out then. Oh, Margot!" She stopped short, peering tragically back over the edge of the trail. " Where's the coffee pot? I couldn't even take care of that. I must have just let go of it. Isn't that dreadful?"

Margot laughed at her. " Well, I don't see just how you could ever have climbed way up here lugging that big coffee pot."

But Tim refused to be comforted. " That's the very last straw," she declared. " You saved the bag of crackers. There they are, right under your arm, Margot. You were brave just by instinct. And you didn't even lose the cheese."

" Fine, maybe we'll need both if we get lost. Come along and forget the coffee pot. But I really do think you could play the game now. Tim, where do you coffee pot? When did you coffee pot last, old dear?"

Tim had to smile a little, but her face was pretty sober. "You can make a joke of it, but all the same, we almost burned up down there, and it's not my fault we didn't. We'd have been suffocated by now at least, at the very least, Margot, and you saved us and got us up here by keeping your head. I'll never forget this as long as I live."

"I wish you'd stop standing there making speeches about it when we've got to find our way out. Here, eat some crackers and feel better." Margot stuffed several into Tim's hand. "Which way out, scout?"

Without replying Tim started up the steep rocky trail again toward the ridge. Her morale was badly shaken, and her high opinion of Katherine Campbell McLean. She had always believed more or less privately that she knew the best way to do anything, and it was a shock to discover that she had made a serious mistake that might have cost them both their lives. She glanced back at Margot who called cheerily,

"Keep on going straight ahead, and don't look back."

It was good advice for the trail became hard to find at all over the hard, rocky ground, but finally they came out on the ridge motor highway, and now Tim realized how far they had travelled trying to find Mr. Watson and his fire fighters. Margot sat down with relief on a rock and started to take off her riding boots. "I feel as if I'd tramped twenty miles," she said. But Tim was not looking at her. Scrambling up over the edge of the road about a stone's throw from them were two strange figures, bearded and wild looking, but Tim recognized them at first sight. The fire had driven something besides rabbits and gophers ahead of it in the race for life. The old professor and Jim Quinn sat down side by side by the road, and leaned for support against each other.

"Who are they?" asked Margot curiously. "How queer they look."

"Don't you know? Everybody thought they were lost hunting gold, and there they are! That's Sallie Jane's husband, Jim, and Sam's a professor from Indiana. We'd better go and rescue them, Margot. This is very exciting news and we'll find ourselves in the front page news of the Frisbee *Outlook*."

Tim started off happily toward the two wearied prospectors, and Margot felt sorry that the coffee was all gone when she saw their gaunt, half-starved faces.

CHAPTER XI

THEY shared what was left of the crackers and cheese between Jim and the professor. The old man was so utterly exhausted that he dozed off on Jim's shoulder while Tim tried to find out where they had been for so long while everyone hunted for them.

" How's Sallie Jane? " asked Jim at once.

" She's ever so much better since you went away even though she's worried over you terribly, but I guess it made her work all the harder to keep her mind off her troubles. Where have you been? "

" Clear over to the other side of the range, and we found the queerest bones you ever saw in your life. I helped dig some of them out, and we were trying to bring a few along to prove our find, but the fire caught us and they're all burned up now. Never thought we'd get through alive."

" I know, we got caught too, down in the canyon. What kind of an animal did the bones belong to, Jim? "

Jim scratched his head and appeared deeply

puzzled. "Mammoth, that's what they were, mammoth."

"There aren't any mammoths this far south, are there, Margot? They must have belonged to a big lizard."

"Do lizards have tusks?" exclaimed Jim indignantly, and the professor roused long enough to murmur, "Certainly not," and he went right back to sleep like the Dormouse, Tim thought.

"Everyone thought you might find gold," Margot said, and there came a curious intent look in Jim's pale blue eyes.

"No, no, we were just after bones," he insisted. "And I can tell you that we're mighty glad to have escaped alive out of that fiery furnace down there."

Tim was wondering how they could all get back to the rangers' cabin when there came the sound of a car puffing along the ridge road, coming up the steep curves in first. Probably it would be Custer or Slim, she thought thankfully, but it was not the same car, she saw as soon as it appeared on the summit. And she had to look twice before she recognized the smoke-grimed, grinning driver.

" Hello," he called. " Where did you all come from? "

Tim hurried to meet him as he stopped the car. " Oh, Don, we've found the professor and Jim, and they're just all in from exhaustion after coming through the fire. We got caught too, down in the canyon, carrying coffee to the men, but Margot saved us."

" Well, I sent in the first alarm. I saw the fire when it started way down Lookout Canyon, and I rode to the electric light plant and told them, and we 'phoned Dave, then I called up Joe and we got everything started."

He looked so satisfied and proud of himself that Tim could only stand and look at him with her eyelashes quivering from silent scorn. " You would go and play wonderful all by yourself, Don McLean. How did the fire start? "

" Smouldering for two days from the last one. I have to be pushing along because I'm carrying supplies to Dave. Don't you all want a ride? "

" We might," Tim said loftily. " Seeing that we've all escaped with our lives from the fire while you've been scooting up and down being Dave's messenger boy. We were almost suffo-

cated, that's all, and the professor is half dead.
If your Imperial Beeswax can stop long enough
to give us assistance, we would thank you for
it."

"You had no business coming over here at
all," Don grumbled. "It's no place for girls."

"I suppose you're chief fire warden for the
whole state by now. Do you know that Joe
sent Dick Thorpe to patrol the main motor
road? He's on Buckskin." Tim couldn't resist telling this, and was rewarded by the gleam
in Don's eyes even though he did look indifferent.
Perhaps he wouldn't boast so much now about all
he had done, she thought, as Jim helped Don
get the old man into the rear seat of the car.
Margot and Tim had to climb in beside him, and
take care of him, but Tim braced him nicely in
one corner so he wouldn't fall over on them, and
Don drove on to where he was to meet Dave.

He came striding toward them with his usual
smile, but looking as if he had been through all
the wars. The fire was pretty well under control
now; it had had its last run when it met Slim's
backfire. Dave was keeping a few lookouts here
and there overnight. He glanced from Don to

the girls in the car and at Jim and the professor. "Where did you find them, Don?" he asked curiously.

"Don never found them, we did, Mr. Watson," protested Tim. "We've been carrying coffee and crackers to the men down the canyon, and we almost got burned to cinders, and we owe you a new coffee pot. Then when we came out on top of the ridge we found Jim and the old man half dead where they'd escaped too."

"Howdy, Dave," Jim waved his hand carelessly. "Got caught like a pair of gophers. Lost our outfit and horses and everything. In luck to be alive. I believe you just started that fire to smoke us out and find out where we were."

Dave laughed and scratched his head. "Wish I'd thought of it sooner, Joe, it would have saved Sallie Jane a pile of worry. You better all go back to the cabin, and I'll send Dick to join you. He did mighty fine work, that boy, and as for Don here, I'm going to make him my deputy ranger."

"Well," sighed Tim later, after they had delivered Jim and the professor over to Joe, "there goes another mystery. I was positive they were both hunting secret gold and had found out more than they wanted to tell, and now I guess it was only bones after all. There comes Dick now, so we can all go home together. I suppose Tumpy will nearly die when she finds out he's been patrolling, won't she?"

"It won't matter because Father will be glad he did it." Margot smiled happily at Dick as he rode over to join them. They all started down the ridge trail which Don said would take them to the edge of the desert in much quicker time than the way they had come. "Well, Dick," Margot said, "you wanted some real adventure out here, and you surely got it, didn't you? Wait till Tumpy sees you."

"I've had a corking time," replied Dick calmly. "Where were you two girls?"

Tim launched into a full description of how they had been lost in the fire zone when the wind turned, and what Margot had done. Dick nodded. "She's a good scout," he said briefly. Don came riding after them and soon caught up on Dusty.

"Gee, I wish I had a good swim," he said. "I feel baked. We've got a pretty good swimming pool up on our place, Dick, if you want to come over some time, or stop in when we get back."

"Thanks, I'd like to." It was all said very simply, but to the girls, it was the first pact of friendship between their brothers, and Tim smiled knowingly at Margot behind the boys' backs. They rode on in pairs, excepting where the trail narrowed, and Don took another short cut down over a beautiful mesa. Cottonwoods grew on it and gave plenty of shade, and the grass was fresh and green excepting where great piles of rock mounted up at the sides like the dry bed of some old cataclysmic torrent. They were riding along chatting when suddenly in the distance they heard the whinny of a horse. The ponies' heads went up alertly, and they answered it, stepping uneasily now, and hesitating.

"Just one of Dave's boys, probably, stationed over here," Don remarked. But as they came farther out on the mesa they saw Pablo's Indian pony advancing eagerly to meet them, but not a sign of Pablo anywhere.

"Oh, it's Pinto," Tim cried. "Don, catch him." And she explained to Margot and Dick all about how the Mexican boy had been missing from the ranch for a couple of days. "He must be right around here somewhere." She sent out a long-drawn call, and both boys whistled shrilly. The ponies stared and switched their long tails, but there came no answering hail from anywhere around them. "I'm sure he can hear us, and is just hiding and watching until we're gone," Tim declared.

Don caught Pinto's bridle and slung it up over his shoulder. "That's all right," he said. "It's a long way for him to walk back."

"But you can't leave him stranded without his pony," Dick protested. "Something may have happened to him."

But Don had started off with Pinto trailing contentedly along beside Dusty. They had hardly reached the other side of the mesa where they were to take the down trail to the edge of the desert when the lone figure of Pablo appeared suddenly from a clump of brush half-way up the rocks. He crawled out and came running after them angrily, calling to Don to let his pony loose. Don only grinned back at him and kept right on going. "I told you he was hiding some place. I know how to make him show himself."

" You no take my pony," Pablo cried fiercely as he caught up with them. He tried to seize Pinto's bridle, but Don wheeled Dusty about like a polo pony and Pinto followed suit.

"Listen, if you want this pony, you're going to climb right up in the saddle, and ride along home with us," Don said flatly. " Who does this pony belong to anyway? Father lets you ride him, but you've got to stick around the ranch and do your work, not trail off for two days playing around. What have you been doing up here? Why weren't you over helping fight fire with Dave? "

" Fire no good," Pablo said sullenly. " Fire drive snakes away."

" What have you been doing up here, Pablo? " Tim demanded severely. Margot was surprised to hear the way they both talked to the tall, fierce looking young Mexican, but Pablo evidently knew how to take Tim's scolding, for he looked up at her with a sudden flashing grin of good humor. " Catching much-a snakes," he said.

" I don't believe you. Snakes." Her tone was withering. " What did you want snakes for? "

" Much-a snake," he repeated eagerly.

" Catch-a rattlesnake. Sell to man in Oro for skin, for poison medicine. Get one dollar for rattlesnake."

" Aren't you wonderful? " Tim said. " Won't they bite you, Pablo? "

Pablo smiled proudly and shrugged his shoulders. " Snake no bite Indian."

" But you're only half Indian. I should think they'd find a Mexican spot somewhere." Again the expressive, nonchalant shrug of Pablo's brown shoulders. He liked Tim, but he scowled when Don spoke to him.

" Where are your snakes? Show them to me."

Don was still suspicious that the boy was not telling the truth, but Pablo started off at once toward the place where he had been hiding. When he came back he carried carefully balanced in his hands two large flat Mexican baskets of finely woven grasses with rounded covers tied firmly in place. He squatted on the ground before them, and untied one half-way, peering inside and making a peculiar hissing, yet caressing sound with his tongue pressed to his upper teeth. Instantly there was a visible stirring in the two baskets, and an answering hiss. Pablo knelt

lower, and looked inside, his eyes bright and half
closed. He made a soft sound that was musical
like the humming of katydids, then he began to
sway slowly from side to side moving his hands
in rhythmic time. They watched him, fascinated,
until he had finished, and tied the covers closely
down again. Then he stood straight up with
folded arms, very calm and dignified, having
demonstrated that he was telling the truth.

Don tossed him Pinto's bridle. " All right,
you win, but mind you turn up at the ranch.
I'll tell Father and Tom we saw you up here, and
you can deliver the snakes in Oro, but show up
for work to-morrow morning sure, or there'll be
plenty trouble."

" I don't see how you catch the snakes," Dick
said in an easy, friendly way that caught Pablo's
attention as he stood muttering to himself after
Don's warning."

" No catch-a snake," he answered coolly.
" Snake come to me."

He picked up his baskets and walked away,
leading Pinto.

" Nice, pleasant sort of person to have around,"
Margot said as they rode away. " I'd be afraid

to talk to him as you do, Tim, for fear he'd hide his pets in my blankets some night."

" Oh, Pablo's all right, only he's lazy and hates to work. Estrella told me he was out hunting snakes, but I didn't believe her. And the Indians have some way of catching rattlesnakes that they'll never tell anyone. Father and Tom were at the big Snake Dance one year, and they said the Indian medicine men charm their snakes just the way the fakirs do in India. Anyway, I'm glad we found Pablo, for two reasons, because he thinks he's so everlastingly smart about not letting anyone know what he's doing, and because I was afraid he might be out hunting something else, and if I caught him snooping around after any of my secrets or Don's, I'd take his pony away from him and let him walk home, wouldn't you, Don? "

" Sure," Don agreed.

" You've got a nice sweet disposition, Tim," Dick remarked. " If my sister were like you, I'd disown her."

" Don't try and make believe that you ever manage me," laughed Margot. " I'd just like to see you try it, old dear."

" Don't you always do everything I tell you to?" Dick teased her with lazy good humor.

" Certainly not. I'm clever enough to make you think that you're having your own way, and I get mine just the same."

" Don't quarrel, children," Tim interposed. " Be glad we're not two perfectly good cooked sisters lying back there in Lookout Canyon. I've wanted to quarrel with Don all day long, and when I saw him show up on the ridge road I was so glad I almost fell on his neck with joy. They're terribly aggravating, but brothers are pretty good to have around sometimes. Aren't they, Margot?"

" Sometimes," Margot agreed, smiling over at Don, as they saw the end of the trail at the edge of the desert ahead of them.

CHAPTER XII

THE unexpected arrival of Jim Quinn and the professor stirred Frisbee with mild excitement and speculation. When the story of the rescue had spread about, Jim took up his headquarters in Sam's store and held forth to all willing hearers on his adventures. The old man was ill from shock and exhaustion, but Jim made up for both of them. Tim told him he ought to stop talking and go to work, with Sallie Jane cooking her young life away over in Mrs. Barney's boarding house, but it did not impress him. Jim loved to romance about himself and pose as a picturesque figure about the little town, but his wings were clipped when the professor recovered sufficiently to realize that Jim was taking all the credit and glory of the expedition away from him.

Tim visited him personally, as soon as Sam told her he was up. Sam had sheltered and befriended him ever since his return, and Tim found him bolstered up in a big camp rocker out on

Mrs. Sam's side porch in the warm sunshine, so she sat down on the top step to chat with him. Before she had finished, the professor had told her how Jim had misled him into thinking he was anxious to go and hunt for prehistoric remains too, but when they reached the lonely mountain region beyond the ridge, Jim had proposed that they become partners and share alike since he was giving the professor the benefit of his time and experience.

"Partners in what?" said the professor. "That is what I asked him, and to my utter amazement he said the gold mine I was after, and the more I explained and protested that I was not a gold seeker, the more he insisted that I was trying to conceal from him the real reason for my trip. Thus, you see, we disagreed."

"Naturally," Tim responded eagerly. "I always knew that Jim was just following you to find out something. Then what happened?"

"Well, he never believed me, no matter how much I explained to him the object of my search. He was certain I was deceiving him, and that I had some secret plan to find gold. He could not see that I was seeking something far more precious than gold, to wit: knowledge." He gazed over the rims of his glasses at Tim's serious face as she gazed up at him, and Tim nodded understandingly. " I was seeking for the buried remains of past ages and peoples, fascinating research into the remote periods when the desert was a great sea, and these mountains were the haunts of unimagined monsters."

" Oh, I can't help but think how Sandy would love to just sit and listen to you talk," sighed Tim. " You must meet him before you go away, Professor. Only he really believes there is gold over in the mountains."

" Possibly." The old man nodded his head without special interest. He looked so gaunt and comical as he sat in the deep chair, wrapped in the blanket, with one of Sam's old gray flannel shirts on, and his gray hair tousled into an aggressive curly crest on top of his head, that Tim felt sorry for him, he seemed at once so forlorn and yet so hopeful.

" Of course, I shall return another year," he said cheerfully, " since I have seen with my own eyes that I am right. We travelled to a lofty mountain top with inaccessible sides to the north, but from there I looked down upon the most beautiful hidden lake, blue as the sky ——"

"That is Bluewater Lake," Tim interrupted. "Sandy knows all about it. I really think that you got the wrong guide, because if you only could have had Sandy instead of Jim, Sandy would have taken you anywhere at all. Sandy says he knows the whole Southwest just like a book, all the deserts and mountains, and everything. He told me once he knows every trail through the Horseshoe Range. You just ought to hear him tell about buried cities and lost rivers and caves."

"Indeed," the professor looked interested. "Who is this Mr. Sandy?"

"He is a very great friend of mine and of my brothers, but most people call him a desert rat, if you know what that means. I don't think it is a good name at all, but I suppose Sandy really is a desert rat because he's always lived way out in the desert in a crazy old shack that he built himself, and he doesn't work at anything specially, but if you'd like to meet him, I'll be glad to bring him up to see you the next time he comes here to Sam's for his supplies."

"I shall be charmed," the professor answered with great dignity. "It is a privilege to meet anyone who contributes even an iota to one's fund of general knowledge."

"Well, I know Sandy can do that, and he loves to talk. I will surely bring him," Tim promised. She went back into the store feeling much better and walked over to the little post office window while Jim stopped his talking to glance around at the slim, jaunty little figure in tan linen blouse and old riding trousers. He wondered why she had been out talking so long to the professor.

Sam handed out a letter to her postmarked Buffalo.

"That's the one you're after, isn't it?" he said. "When's your mother expected home again, Tim?"

"First of June so she can see me graduate," Tim replied. "I wish she were home now. I'm just sick and tired of nothing but boys around me. Got any nice fresh potato chips, Sam? Give me ten cents' worth, and some sweet pickles, and a box of baking powder. It's awfully hot in town, isn't it? I wouldn't live here for anything;

why, it's just as cool and breezy as can be up on the mesa."

"Fine," Sam agreed. "I hear you 'n' Dave put the canyon fire out between you."

"Well, we got some of the gophers out of their holes." Tim laughed and picked up her groceries. "Good-bye, Sam, take good care of the professor."

"Got Pablo home again too, didn't you?"

"Oh, yes, he was only snake hunting." She sauntered out of the store with Jim still eyeing her, and for a while he was unusually silent until he said casually that every last one of the McLean youngsters thought they knew too much, and especially that last one.

"Can't say anything against Tim around here," Sam told him flatly. "Besides, she's been mighty good to Sallie Jane all the time you were lost in the shuffle over yonder, Jim. I wouldn't talk against Tim if I were you. She's sort of a town fixture."

Jim subsided, but watched Tim as she walked down the opposite side of the street to the drug store. Her one personal extravagance on Saturdays was a marshmallow sundae, and she loved to buy one down at Mr. Herrara's drug store after she had finished her regular shopping. All the school children called him Mr. Hurrah and on Saturdays he was usually asleep in the little room off the store, while Benito, his eldest son, waited on customers. Benito fixed up the sundae for Tim, and topped it off with an extra sprinkling of delicious chopped walnuts and a cherry.

"Benito," Tim said after a few moments, while she ran her long handled spoon slowly around the edge of the ravishing concoction, "do you know anyone down in Oro who would buy any rattlesnakes?"

"Sure, Andy Millard buys plenty, kills 'em, skins 'em, sells skins for shoe leather, fancy pocket-books, all kinds of things. Why?"

"Oh, dear." Tim sighed as she leaned both elbows on the counter while she sipped the cream. "I'm just discouraged, all my best mysteries go to pieces, Benito. I thought rattlesnakes were only good for their poison. Life is terribly matter of fact, isn't it? Pablo's been away from the ranch, and we thought he wasn't coming back, and Don and I found him catching rattlesnakes over in the mountains, and he said he sold them to someone down in Oro."

"What did you suppose he was going to do with them?" Benito grinned at her. "Pablo knows rattlesnakes like the Indians. He can charm them."

"Exactly, I know it," Tim said quickly, "and that's just why I thought ——"

She stopped short. It would never do to tell Benito she thought maybe Pablo was out practicing so he could charm the rattlesnakes that guarded the hidden gold up in the blind canyon Sandy had told her about.

"He's all right. I went to school with Pablo," Benito talked on, not noticing her. "He's got lots of sense, that boy, Indian sense, only he's queer. He never forgives anyone who's mean to him. He can remember it for years and pay back a grudge, and that's Indian too."

"Well, he certainly hasn't any grudge to pay back at our ranch," Tim protested; "my father's awfully good to him, and the boys tease him some, but they all like him, only he should not run away and neglect his work."

"Pablo likes all of you McLeans. I tell you

who he don't like, that's Jim Quinn. Once Jim struck him over the head with a leather quirt when Pablo wouldn't catch his pony for him, but Pablo did not catch the pony. That was four years ago, and if you don't believe me, just watch him look at Jim Quinn some day, just like a rattlesnake looks before it springs."

" Really? Why, I always thought that Pablo and Jim were mixed up together trying to find out the old professor's gold mine secret, and that was why he ran away from the ranch."

Benito shook his head. " Ever see a king snake fight a rattler? Some day Pablo says he is going to pay Jim back for that quirt cut. If I were Jim Quinn, I would move away from Frisbee."

" My, Benito, I'm so glad I stopped in here for this sundae, because here you've given me a brand new thriller just as my best one petered out." Tim rose from the stool. " Now tell me this one: do you believe there's any gold at all left around here? "

" Plenty. My father says there is gold all around us common as pebbles, and the Indians know where it is. People laugh and say that is an old story, but it is the truth."

"Then why on earth doesn't he hunt for it instead of running a drug store?"

Benito laughed and showed his white teeth as he shrugged his shoulders. "I guess he like to go to sleep and have folks bring the money to him over the counter, easier than to dig it himself."

"But you'd never want to stay here forever, would you, and be a druggist too?"

"Me?" He stopped laughing and straightened his shoulders. "I am going to the aviation school this summer. Every day I go out to watch the mail plane when it passes over here. I know the pilot's name, Bob Darnton. Once I talked to him down at San Diego, and he told me where I could go to school and learn."

"Well," Tim said heartily, "you've given me a lot of interesting things to think about, Benito, and here I never dreamt you ever knew anything except about drug stores. Good-bye, I've got to rush this baking powder home, and I forgot all about it."

"That's all right, I always thought you looked kind of funny too," Benito answered, and Tim walked out of the store, not knowing whether to laugh or be angry at him. She couldn't think of any other immediate sources of information for the moment, so she mounted Chapo and rode on home.

In the kitchen Estrella greeted her with a prolonged and fiery scolding for staying so long, but Tim did not even wait to listen, just dropped the baking powder on the table by the door, and ran down to the corral, where she thought she might find Don and tell him all her news, about Jim and the old professor and what Benito had told her about Pablo. It always seemed as if, when Tim went to town, she came back full of news, but when she had finished telling everything, Don was only interested in the name of the air pilot, Bob Darnton. The rest he thought was just the old professor's ravings, and Benito's gossip. He glanced up at the clear blue sky overhead and then at the shadow of the nearest tree.

"Most noon. He'll pass over any time now."

"Will he? Oh, I'm going to signal to him." Tim hunted about for something bright enough to attract attention, and finally raced back to the house and found a bright orange silk scarf.

On her way back to the corral she stopped short. "He'll never see me down here on account of the trees," she thought. "I must stand on something to make me high up in the air." The low buildings around the corral were altogether too inconspicuous, but the bright tiled roof of the ranch house caught her eye. "Of course, I'll stand on the house," she called down to Don.

Estrella was busy baking when she caught the noise of strange footfalls on the tiled roof overhead. Sometimes the eucalyptus dropped its pointed seed pods on the tiles, and often the cats liked to stroll up there or the inquisitive mocking birds would hop around, but this was a heavier footed animal and Estrella listened intently before she went over to her own chest in a corner and produced an old rusty pistol. It was not even loaded, but she took it in her hand and stole out to where she could get a good look at the prowler. Just then there came the singing whirr of a motor up in the air, and the big silver gray mail plane came humming out of the south and pointed its course straight for the mesa. And from the roof she heard Tim's long drawn hail:

" Hel-lo, Bob Darnton! Hel-lo!"

He couldn't possibly hear her, but Tim waved the golden silk scarf back and forth eagerly, and just as the plane was overhead it fluttered out like a long banner over her head, and the plane dipped in return salute.

" He saw me," Tim cried triumphantly as she came to the edge of the roof and climbed down the rose trellis. " Did you see him, Estrella? He did that just to let me know that he saw the scarf. He dipped down just as though he were bowing."

" I see too much-a," said Estrella haughtily. " You great big-a girl up on roof like a monkey, what your mama say, huh?"

" Just what did you expect me to stand on, Estrella?" Tim asked with dignity. " There wasn't time for me to climb a tree, was there, and anyway, he'd never have seen me if I had. You're too fussy about me. Mother wouldn't say a word because she understands me, and you never do. You like the boys and you always stand up for them no matter what they do, but the minute it's me, you have seventeen fits."

Instantly Estrella mellowed at the breaking

note in Tim's voice. " Ah, *mia pepita, carina,*
Estrella's little baby cabbage ——"

" Don't you dare call me a little baby cabbage
again, I just won't stand it, Estrella," stormed
Tim. " It isn't a pet name in English and I've
told you that over and over. Don't you ever
remember anything?"

" Nice-a little baby *conejita,*" smiled Estrella
archly.

" No, I'm not a little baby rabbit either." Tim
stalked back to Don indignantly, but found him
drawing a design of something on the ground
with a pointed stick. " What are you doing?"
she asked. " Didn't you see me make Bob Darnton salute me?"

" Sure I did. I don't suppose he ever even
saw the ranch before. Now look here, there's
plenty of good level land back of the corral along
the mesa if it's only cleared up a bit; and I'm
going to ask Dad to let us have it for a flying
field."

" Aren't you wonderful? Just who thought
of that first?" Tim stood looking at him with
scorn. " I don't suppose you ever remember the
day we were riding back from Sandy's, and I

told you I was going to do that very thing, and you said Father wouldn't let me?"

Don's blue eyes twinkled teasingly as he looked back at her.

"Did you? All right, then, we'll make it together, but you have to work fifty-fifty, and help cart off the rocks and brush."

Mollified, Tim relented enough to sit down on the ground beside him and look over what he was doing. He marked out a small plan of what the field would be like, and Tim asked how they would let the pilot know it was made expressly for him to land on.

"Fall on, you mean, he'd never use it unless he had to make a forced landing," Don told her. "We'll write him a letter down to San Diego, and tell him about it."

"And we can hang out a lantern at night the way Sandy does. In the daytime I think it would be splendid to have great big letters painted white and made of wood laid out on the field like a message from Mars—remember how we read about that—and it can say FALL HERE."

"You mean LAND HERE, the other might

make him nervous. I want to give it a real name like any other landing field. Perhaps Oro or Frisbee will take the hint and build a real one."

"McLean Field is really the right name for it, the family may as well have the credit, don't you think so, Don? Sandy will approve because he's interested in Bob Darnton too. Do you suppose he'll ever appreciate all we're trying to do for him?"

"Well, he certainly will the first time he finds himself slipping with nothing but the desert and mountains under him, and no place to land. I'll ask Dad when he comes home to-night, and if Tom will keep still and not speak up and say it can't be done, we'll go ahead and do it."

Tim perched herself on her favorite seat, the top rail of the corral bar gate, and regarded her brother with thoughtful and reluctant admiration. "You know, Don, I just get all comfortably settled into believing that you'll never be the same to me again, and I don't like you at all, and then you turn around and do something really nice and wonderful. I thought that you had forgotten all about having a landing field on our mesa."

" Just because I didn't go around talking about it to everybody like a girl? "

" You just mean that for Margot and me, and I think you're just horrid, Don McLean."

Don laughed with deep chuckles of enjoyment. " If you don't watch out, we'll be scrapping in another minute because we're hungry and snappy as turtles. Come on and eat."

" Will you call it Campbell Field after me? " asked Tim.   " That's after great-grandmother Campbell too, and I'd rather please the family than Frisbee, wouldn't you? "

" It should be named for a hero! "

" Then call it Darnton Field. It will make Bob feel like a hero and most of them don't get a chance before they die. I mean the ones they name places after. I want to get all my medals and honors while I'm still alive."

Estrella appeared in the doorway of the kitchen calling to them to come up for dinner. Saturdays they always had dinner at noon, and Tim was good and hungry. As they walked up to the house Pablo came strolling around the corner of the patio, but saw them, and immediately turned around and walked the other way.

CHAPTER XIII

THE landing field on the mesa soon became a reality after Mr. McLean had given his consent. But even he did not realize what a practical field Don and Tim had in mind and were capable of making. Of course, as Tim said, it took a lot of time, but as soon as Don's friends at school heard what he was doing, they came trooping over to help, and then Neil begged to come in on the fun too, with his younger crowd.

Even Dave Watson rode over to look at the field on his usual Sunday morning visit to the ranch, and pronounced it a fine plan. He gave the children good advice on cutting and stacking their brush and burning it safely, and also on making a heavy drag of branches for the ponies to pull over the cleared ground and sweep it clean.

One afternoon as they were working hard during the short time they had free after school, Tim and Don were surprised to find old Sandy mounted on Cleo, riding up the long road from the canyon. He turned in behind the corral and came out to where they were working, and surveyed the great flat tableland. It stretched back of the ranch proper for nearly a mile, and the field was not even cleared of half its brush yet, but it began to show what they were striving for.

"Why didn't you just start a good brush fire and burn it off, much easier than dragging off all that stuff by the roots," Sandy said, but Tim assured him they'd had enough of brush fires and they didn't mind clearing it off this way one bit for safety's sake.

"How are you going to notify that flier that this here field is here all ready and waiting his convenience?"

"We'll write him a letter. Benito Cornejo knows him personally and we can explain everything to him that way. Do you think one lantern is large enough to give a signal light for such a big field, Sandy? Don thought we'd better hang out two or even three."

"One's enough," Sandy pronounced gravely. "It only takes one moon to light up the whole heavens at night, doesn't it, and a ship's light ain't a mite bigger than your lantern. From up there where he is a lantern light will gleam like a lighthouse out on this mesa. I've got another old ship's lantern back in the shack some place that I picked up in a curio shop down in San Pedro one day, and I'll donate it to this enterprise. Warranted not to expire when the old ship rolls too. I'll bring it up to you next time I travel this way, and tell Don to stick up a pole for it to hang on. Seen anything of that old enemy of mine, Jim Quinn?"

"He's sitting around Sam's store, not doing one tap of work and talking his head off about all the things that he and the professor discovered."

"Don't believe they ever found so much as the little toe of even a prehistoric chameleon let alone any monsters. Jim's just talking, burning wind as usual."

"Oh, Sandy," Tim said eagerly, "I do believe the professor though, even if I couldn't Jim, wouldn't you? He told me that they did discover some kind of remains."

"Remains?" repeated Sandy scornfully. "Why, say, if I was to begin and tell you the authentic remains that I've looked at with my own eyes, you could fill a whole history book with it. I've found caves in mountains with members of dead and gone tribes and forgotten races sitting around easy like with household utensils set out handy like, and the bones of the last meal flung in a corner. I've been in the deserted homes of the cliff dwellers, places no one else has found yet, and did I disturb them for the sake of the public's idle curiosity? I should say not. I walked out and left them just as they were out of respect for what didn't concern me. My sole motto has always been to mind my own business, and I don't believe in so much as touching remains. Let them stay right where they fell, say I, professor or no professor, and I'd tell him the same."

"Would you, Sandy?" Tim looked at him in a worried way. "You see, I've already told him that you know more about such things than anyone else in the entire state and he believes me, and he's expecting you to call and talk with him."

"Well, if he wants to take a squint at me, I wouldn't go so far as to disappoint him," answered Sandy cheerfully. "I know I'm picturesque, and more than that, I'm obliging. If as you say, Tim, he's a friend of yours, I'm willing to drop in and say hello to him, and I certainly shall do so the next time I drop in at Sam's for a side of bacon and a sack of corn meal. But that ain't saying that I'd tell him any of my secrets."

"Oh, he wouldn't expect you to, Sandy, just be pleasant and sociable to him, and cheer him up, because he's awfully discouraged, and he did get hold of some kind of remains, and now Jim's talking so much that he's taking all the glory away from him."

"The remains they found are probably the bones of old Bill Woolsey's mule team that wandered off and got lost over in the Horseshoe Range about forty-two years ago. I could have told them that much if they'd asked me. I think less of Jim Quinn's opinion on any subject at all than I do of the feller that writes the almanac, and that's saying some. I wouldn't ask Jim to a coyote's funeral. He's been contradicting all of my predictions ever since he come out here to Frisbee, and some day I'm going to explain to him my opinion of one Mr. Quinn."

"I'd love to hear you do it," Tim said fervently. " If you'll just call on the professor and talk nice to him, it will cut Jim all up and hurt his pride terribly now."

" It will, will it? I'll travel that way to-morrow." Sandy urged Cleo on her ambling way, and departed again down the canyon road. It would be a good thing, Tim thought as she watched him ride away, for the poor old professor to have all the friends and well wishers he could get just now, and she went back to her work contentedly.

At the end of three weeks, the children felt they had done all they could to make the landing field complete. Don wrote the letter that was to notify Bob Darnton, and Tim got his address from Benito,—Mr. Robert L. Darnton, Air Mail Pilot, San Diego, Cal. Don took great pains with the letter although most of it was suggested by Tim. They read it over together when it was finished:

" DEAR MR. DARNTON:

We believe that it would be very dangerous for you to fall over this country, and we have turned the mesa back of our ranch into a landing

184 THE DOOR IN THE MOUNTAIN

field for you in case of emergency. Please feel
free to use it any time you have to. We will hang
a lantern out at night, and in the daytime if you
will look down at the field when you fly over the
McLean ranch north of Frisbee in Las Flores
Canyon, you will notice a cleared field and on it
these words in white letters,

LAND HERE.

Wishing you the best of luck always,
Your friends,
THE MCLEANS."

There was a long discussion on how the letter should be signed, but finally the clan spirit
of the McLeans prevailed. Don said since it was
on Mr. McLean's land, and Neil had helped and
Tom had helped make the wooden letters stay on
the ground without getting all crooked, it was
only fair to sign the family name, so the letter
was sent off this way.

They waited anxiously for several days and
Tim watched the airplane pass, thinking perhaps
that Bob would devise some sensational way of
communicating with them. It would have been
so exciting to have a letter thrown from the
plane, weighted and aimed for the mesa, but

when it came, it was duly stamped and passed out through Sam's post office window to Tim's eager hands. She could hardly wait to get home and share it with Don. It was signed "Yours truly, Bob Darnton," which Tim thought was a little formal considering all they had done for him, but maybe he was shy. She read the letter over Don's shoulder.

"DEAR FRIENDS:

Many thanks for the tip on landing field. We sure need them. I saw the lantern Friday night and wondered what it was for, and Saturday I flew low enough to read the white sign in the field. Looks all right. Hope I don't have to use it, but if I do, I certainly will be much obliged to you all. Best wishes to Benito.

Yours truly,
BOB DARNTON."

"It seems as if he might have written lots more after all the trouble we took for him," sighed Tim. "I wish I knew what he looks like."

"Write back and ask him to send you an autographed picture of himself, make him feel just like Lindy," teased Don.

"Smarty." Tim looked down at him with her

haughtiest air as she perched on a eucalyptus log,
her hands clasped over one knee. She felt proud
of the great cleared oval field on the mesa, although people in Frisbee seemed to think the
McLeans were going a bit too far in making a
private landing field. Sam had told Tim that
while it was all right and mighty kind of them to
do it, still it was a sort of hint to the town to
provide a landing field, and there was folks that
didn't like to be hinted at, they wanted to take
their own time, and landing fields meant town
bonds.

"Yes, and in the meantime the sky is just
sprinkling pilots here and there," Tim retorted.
"I only hope the town takes our hint and all the
other towns too, but I think we've got the best
location. If he's caught in any engine trouble
over the mountains he can just glide right down
to our field."

"Ain't you optimistic?" laughed Sam. "Ever
see a plane in trouble? I have, and they just
drop, that's all, like a shot bird."

Tim was thinking of this now as she gazed at
the field after Don left her. She did hope that
Bob Darnton would never have to fall like a

shot bird somewhere over those mountains or the
desert. Then she heard Margot's voice calling
to her, and jumped up to hurry back to the house.
She had forgotten that the Thorpes were coming over to look at the completed field, and that
Dick was going with the boys on a hike up the
canyon after water puppies.

Estrella was in a kindly mood and Tim found
a tray waiting her with delicious fruit punch on
it and little flat nut and fig cakes that she loved.
She carried the round Chinese tray into Tim's
part of the house, the two rooms at the south
end of the patio, where it was cool and shady,
and set it down between Margot and herself on
the long low couch.

" I like your room, Tim," Margot said as she
sat cross-legged on the red and gray Navajo
blanket that covered the couch. There were low
bookcases between the two windows with little
narrow shelves above, two high backed Hawaiian
chairs of black and cream bamboo, and on the
walls hung an Indian war drum and two Mexican
guitars.

" Tom brought me the drum from San Diego,
and Mother gave me the chairs because I always

loved them in her room, and Father made the
bookcases for me, and I shot the mountain lion.
Don't you like it? It's all so roomy and restful,
and I just won't let the boys come near it."

Margot looked all about her and sighed. "You
have everything you want right here," she said.
"I shouldn't think that you would ever want to
go away."

"But I do," Tim protested, pouring the punch
out in amber glasses. "I want to travel like you
and Dick have, and see things. I've lived right
here all my life, and have only been up camping
in the High Sierras, and gone down to Catalina
of course, and San Pedro and San Diego. I
think I really loved that best on account of the
harbor. Father says some day we may move to
Los Angeles, but I don't want to do that. I'd
rather travel to the islands and China, and everywhere."

"I think this is one of the loveliest places I've
ever lived in. You've been here all your life, so
you don't think so, but it is. May I see the war
drum, please?" Margot held out her arms as
Tim stepped up on a stool and lifted down the
drum and curious stick attached to it from the

hook. The barrel shaped drum was marked over with strange Indian symbols in brightly colored paint, and long thongs of leather strung with red and blue and amber glass beads dangled from either end. The drum stick was of carved wood with a large gourd-shaped end made from a painted bladder tightly stretched over the stick.

"This is modern," Tim told her. "You ought to see some of the Indian relics that they dig up over in Catalina Island, remains of the Channel Indians, nobody knows how long ago. Father said they found the other day a big jar packed with all sorts of things, abalone jewelry and spear heads, around the skeleton of a little girl. They think she must have been a princess, and that was the way they buried her like the slave girl in the Forty Thieves, remember, with all her toys and jewels around her."

"They bury people sitting up like that in Africa too," Margot said. "Aren't we nice and cheerful talking about such things? Tumpy nearly dies when Dick and I start chatting about head hunters and savage burials."

"Wait a minute, I'll show you something beautiful." Tim dove suddenly into a closet, and hauled out an old chest. She threw back the carved top. "This is the wedding chest of the beautiful Donna Elvira Ramirez Marques. I don't know anything about her except her name, and the date, look," she pointed inside the cover where the name was carved deeply, and the date, 1734. "Isn't that wonderful? Father bought it for me at an old auction in San Luis Obispo. I'm sure it was her bridal chest, so I keep all of my treasures in it, coyote teeth and silver bracelets set in turquoise, and moonstones," she kept tossing each article over into Margot's lap, "and this, most of all I love it." She lifted out a white silk Spanish shawl embroidered heavily in white roses, with knotted silk fringe over a foot long. "Mother gave it to me on my thirteenth birthday. Isn't she wonderful? She'd had it for years and years, and always promised it to me. Every year on my birthday she gives me something that I have always longed for."

Margot gazed at the shawl as Tim wrapped it about her like a Mexican girl and danced some tango steps humming the stately air. "I have treasures too," she said, "that belonged to my mother, but my grandmother has them back in

England, so I will have them all some day, but it isn't as if my mother could give them to me herself. Of course I shall love them, but—it's different."

Tim stopped and took off the shawl, then she asked if Margot wouldn't like to go down to the corral and see Tom's new palomino. And while she did not say so directly, Margot knew she meant that it was better not to talk about mothers.

CHAPTER XIV

Ever since he had returned from his rattle-snake hunt, Pablo had avoided the children. He acted resentful and moody as if his pride were very deeply hurt, and he would only talk to Neil. When his work was finished around the corral he would cover his face with his peaked Mexican hat, and lie for hours in the shade of the pepper trees rolled in an old Indian blanket, apparently asleep.

"He's angry over the forest fire, too," Neil said, "because it drove all the snakes deep down in their holes and scorched some, and drove out a lot of others."

Tim thought about the rattlesnakes up in the blind canyon and wished a forest fire would break out there and burn them out. She mentioned it to Don when they were alone, and he told her it was a fine idea, to be sure to tell Dave about it when she saw him, he'd be delighted.

"I don't mean to start one there, goose, only since they do have to burn once in a while, I just wished they might break out some place where they'd do some good. Anyway, you don't care any more, and I do."

"What do you mean, I don't care?" demanded Don. "Just because I don't want everybody to find out about it, and don't drag them over there to help find it the way you do? I've been out to Sandy's and made him draw a map for me all the way from the Splinter to the place from where, he says, the door could be seen. And he said he'd ride over with me and help look for it this Saturday." He looked up, and Tim's face was a study. Without saying a word she turned around and started to walk away. "You can go along if you want to, Tim," he added. "If you'll just swear and promise not to tell anyone about it."

"Isn't that sweet of you, considering it's my secret and I happened to tell you about it."

"You did nothing of the sort. Sandy told us when we were right there together, and it's just as much my secret as it is yours. Gee, I do think girls are crazy the way they think they can say anything or do anything, and get away with it."

"Well, you don't have to be so fussy, do you?

I'm going with you. What time are you starting, and listen, don't think you can get up around
five and go before I'm up. If you do, I'll hide
your best gun and your flashlight, and everything
I can find."

"All right, who cares?" Don said. "What are
you scrapping about, anyway? Get up around
six because we'll be gone all day. We're to meet
Sandy at the Splinter and I told him you'd bring
along something to eat ——"

Tim melted at once into a smile. "Did you,
Don? Then you meant to take me along, didn't
you? I'm sorry for what I said."

"Yes, you are. You'd snap right back at me
if I said a word you didn't like. We're going
to meet Sandy and ride over with him ——"
Don stopped and looked at the figure of Pablo
not fifteen paces away from them, lying under
the pepper trees. " I didn't know he was there."

"Oh, he's sound asleep," Tim answered carelessly. " Be sure and call me as soon as you wake
up in the morning."

Don promised he would and went on up to the
house for some wire he needed on the new aerial
he was putting up, but Tim walked closer to

Pablo, watching him suspiciously. She didn't
see how he could sleep so much, although Estrella
took her siesta after dinner regularly. Tim never
could sleep in the daytime. She thought it was
a sheer waste of time. Pablo seemed to feel that
someone was looking at him, for presently he
rolled over lazily and lifted the hat from his face.
He saw Tim, but did not speak.

"It's a good thing you've got such a good
friend in Benito Cornejo," Tim remarked
pointedly. "I was asking him all about you,
Pablo, and he said he went to school with you,
and he knew the man that you sold snakes to
down in Oro, and that you were all right."

Pablo raised one eyebrow as if to indicate that
he did not care particularly what Benito nor anyone else thought about him. But he did not roll
back to go to sleep, and Tim knew that he was
disposed to listen.

"Sandy likes you too, and you don't have to
act grumpy and angry at me all the time just
because Don and I found you up in the mountains and suggested that you come back to the
ranch and do your work instead of playing
around with those snakes. I suppose now, that

you'll bear a grudge against me for years and years just like you do against Jim Quinn for hitting you with a quirt." She spoke before she thought, but Pablo leaped to his feet, his dark eyes blazing with quick anger, his hands clenched tightly.

"Who tell you that?" he demanded.

"Why, let's see," Tim meditated to gain time. "I heard it somewhere around town. Why on earth are you flaring up like a firecracker over such a simple little thing as that? I don't suppose I should have even mentioned it, only I'm always forgetting a person can't talk to you as if you had real good common sense like other people. Go on back to sleep."

But Pablo strode over to where she stood, and spoke as Estrella did when she was very intense and sombre. "No Mexicano like Jim Quinn. No Indian man like Jim Quinn. He no good, understand?"

"Well, he seems a little unpopular, if that's what you mean," Tim agreed placidly, "but he isn't really out and out bad, Pablo, you can't say that just because he happened to hit you once. Don't you suppose it's just his way, that

he doesn't really mean anything by it? And
you're supposed to forgive your enemies. You
go to church every week and sometimes three
times a day, Pablo, so you ought to remember
at least that. Can't you possibly forgive Jim for
Sallie Jane's sake? Everybody else does, because
she really cares for him, and he's only conceited
and lazy."

Pablo's face was curious. His lips were set in
a tight line, and he merely raised his eyebrow
again just as high as it could possibly go, and
shrugged his shoulders as he walked away without another word.

"All right, don't," Tim called after him. "Be
revengeful and horrid like a—an elephant." For
the moment she couldn't think of anything else
that always remembered grudges and cherished
revenge. She went back to the house thinking
of one of Dave's stories about a circus elephant
that had never forgotten a man who had prodded
him with a long spiked stick, and three years
after when the same circus had played Oro, the
elephant caught sight of the man, and just
reached for him and beat him against a tent pole
until he died.

Revenge was just like that, Tim thought, something that should belong to animals and not to people who could think and who knew the right way. Not that she cared about Jim. He certainly had been cruel to Pablo, but since Sallie Jane loved him she felt that somehow people should try and make the best of Jim. She wondered now whether it was her duty to warn Jim about Pablo's hating him, but on second thought, she decided, no, it was not. She had better keep right out of the trouble. Don always said she was too fond of mixing into other people's affairs, and always wanted a finger in everybody's pie. But perhaps she might just mention it to Sallie Jane the next time she saw her. There couldn't be any harm in doing that, and Sallie Jane would be very grateful to her.

About six-thirty the next morning she and Don rode away to the desert to join Sandy, and arrived at the Splinter in what they thought was good time, but they found Sandy waiting for them, placidly smoking his pipe, with Tony standing patiently by and Powder making wild charges at every gopher within reach.

"Got plenty of time before the shadow falls

at noon due north," Sandy remarked. " Thought maybe we'd enjoy a little snack to eat right here before we cut across to the mountains. Got a little shade to rest in, and I brought a can of water with me that is still cool."

Tony and Cleo were loaded up like pack mules, and Sandy drew forth not only a big can of fresh water, but a coffee can which opened up and revealed what he called a " mess o' beans." Crackers and cheese he contributed also, and Tim produced Estrella's ample lunch of fried cold chicken, tortillas, and " much-a " cake. They ate it all gypsy fashion in the shade of the lone cottonwood that straggled up one side of the Splinter, and after resting until the shadow pointed due north, Sandy took his bearings with great gravity and deliberation, and they started off for the particular mountain he had picked out as the right one with the door in it.

" Not that I have the slightest idea we'll ever be able to get to it in one day," he explained, " but I figured we might ride over and just reconnoiter, so to speak, otherwise prowl around and see where it is and what the dangers and difficulties are. I brought Powder with me because he's

as much death on rattlers as a king snake, which
he ain't by a long shot. And I myself can shoot
backwards and hit any blame rattlesnake this
side of Kingdom Come and make him wish he'd
stayed in his own back yard. I never was afraid
of snakes, and my opinion is that Mister Snake
is just as anxious to get out of your way as you
are out of his, but when he thinks that you're in-
truding and trespassing in his domain, he objects.
Now, if we just step along a little mite we'll
get there sooner. Let 'em have a good run."

The ponies responded gladly, and galloped
over the level ground dodging of their own accord
the clumps of cactus and bayonet plant. The
Horseshoe Range changed from soft amethyst to
rose as they drew nearer. Tim never wearied
of its varying beauty in the golden sunshine when
deep purple cloud shadows passed over its sum-
mits. She lingered purposely behind Sandy and
Don, letting Chapo take his own time after he
had a run to his heart's content, and was content
to go along now at an easy lope. From this distance the mountain wall seemed impassable, but
as they drew closer, Sandy pointed out where the
canyon he was aiming after slashed into the

range. Only a deep cut in the skyline showed at first. There was not a sign of any trail or road leading in from the desert, nothing apparently but the waste land of rock and mesquite and sage as far as the eye could see.

"When I get way off over here, I always feel as if it was just the beginning of the world," declared Sandy. "The first dawn of day and chaos all about me. I shouldn't be at all surprised to behold antediluvian monsters strolling out of them there canyons to greet me, which reminds me, I went up to Sam's and paid a call on your professor, and the old man was glad to see me. He's a mighty fine old customer."

"Oh, I'm so glad you went to see him," Tim exclaimed. "Did you see Jim too?"

"I certainly did, and I walked right past him like he wasn't so much as a boiled stick of macaroni. And I sat and talked with the professor and found out he has a fine mind ranging a good deal like my own on all subjects. I told him I'd like to have him come out and dine with me any time he cared to when he got better, and he said he might if they didn't yank him back to his college. He never came out here after gold or oil.

He's just what he says he is, a nice old bone hunter, only he's got his own name for it. Wait a minute, he wrote it down for me." He dug in his back overall pocket, and fished out a card. Tim reached for it, and read:

" PROFESSOR JEFFERSON R. PAYSON,
Bradley College,
Bradley, Ind."

" That's his name, and I called him Jeff before I left," went on Sandy happily. " He wasn't sent out here after gold, just for these here prehistoric remains, and I respect him for it. He can put up at my shack any time he feels like it, and I told him so."

Tim looked at the shabby, happy old fellow with deep admiration. " You are wonderful, Sandy. Why, you're like a king out here. It's just as if you were the monarch of this whole desert."

" Well, I wouldn't go so far as to say that," replied Sandy modestly, " but I certainly know my Mojave. Now yonder's the way into that blind canyon, and I'm going to take you up a

THE DOOR IN THE MOUNTAIN 203

little way, say a couple of miles or so, but I
wouldn't go any further. And I've brought the
glasses along if you want to take a look."

Tim felt excited and thrilled as they turned
into the rocky canyon trail and rode along between the two towering mountain sides. It was
as Sandy said, primeval in its chaotic immensity;
strange masses of some great upheaval had left
the rock strata in long sweeping drifts of vari-
colored beauty. It all looked so solid, like granite,
but when you came to touch it, it crumbled into
small pieces.

"But mind, this is where you find the copper
and gold and silver," Sandy said. "Liable to
crop out anywhere at all in a country like this.
Folks think it's all petered out, and there won't
be no more gold found, but I tell you it's lying
around waiting for the right one to pick it up.
Trouble is nowadays, it takes so much money to
develop a claim and get the stuff out, most folks
would rather let it alone than bother with it."

Don and Tim were hardly listening to him,
they were so busy watching the sides of the
mountain. "Which side did you say the door is
on, Sandy?" Tim asked eagerly.

"Right as you go in, left as you come out. As I remember it's about three and a half miles long, this canyon, and we can't go up much further on account of no trail. You can see just about what it's all like from here, and this has grown up so in three years since I was here that I hardly know my way. I doubt if you can see the door."

"How far is it?" Tim persisted, watching the left wall eagerly and letting Chapo choose his own way.

"About half-way, maybe more. You see how the dry bed of this creek's widening out, don't you, and how it's getting rockier all the way? Just this fringe of grass and trees along the bank on this side. Live oaks these are and mighty pretty to my way of thinking, and there used to be plenty of game here when I first come out, deer and bear and lion. Where are you going now?"

Tim had slipped down from her saddle and was starting to climb the nearest rocky height on the right side of the creek where they were riding. She had the spy-glass firmly grasped in one hand.

"I'm only going up here above the tree tops

so I can get a good look, Sandy," she called back. " I'm all right."

Don and Sandy waited while she climbed, finding a foothold along the ledges where she could pull herself up, hanging to the bushes and upper ledges for support. Powder insisted on scrambling up after her, breathless and panting, tumbling and slipping, then recovering himself, but keeping right after her until they both came out on top of the rock, and stood there, Tim with her glass levelled at the mountainside opposite.

The canyon wall sloped like the side of a pyramid, its rock ledges making gigantic steps twenty and thirty feet high. As far as she could see there was just the same stretch of wilderness, rugged rock and barren sun-baked ground, and still more rocks as far into the canyon as she could see.

When she had scrambled down she told Don what she had seen and for the first time they both realized what an almost hopeless quest it was ever to hope to find the door. But Sandy took the glass from her leisurely, and adjusted it, focussing it on a line far above the trees even where they were standing on the creek trail. And all

at once he trained it on one spot steadily, looking
long and intently before he lowered it.

"You can't see it, can you, Sandy?" Tim
asked eagerly.

But Sandy took his own time, levelling the
glass again and scrutinizing with even more care
the particular place in the mountain wall opposite that he had discovered. Both Don and
Tim tried to follow the direction the glass pointed
in, but could see nothing at all but rocks and
straggly trees here and there.

"Well," he said finally, as he dropped it lower
and wiped the back of his mouth with his hand.
"I've found a landmark that I can recall being
close to the door. It ain't the door itself, but just
you gaze through this glass till you find a crooked
black pine growing up out of the canyon against
the side of that rock wall. Looks for all the
world like a big serpent crawling up the rock
with its roots exposed like that, and I think it's
been growing like that for generations, but I remember it, and I know it's just north of the door.
There ain't any trail that climbs that high that
I know of, and that's the mysterious part of it.
Whoever used it, or made it, came down a nar-

row and dangerous trail from the top of the mountain, and in that way, he probably avoided the rattlesnakes."

"But how did you ever get up to it?" asked Don puzzled.

"Never said I ever got clear up to it, did I? I said I'd seen it, and so I have, before there was so much growth up there, plain as the nose on your face, and it's a real door built right bang into the side of that mountain and I can swear to it, timbered and clamped like any other door."

"Could you see the trail that came down from the top of the mountain?"

"No, I couldn't, but the Indian told me about it, the one I told you I saved, remember? And beyond that mountain as the bird flies, is Bluewater Lake."

"Then the professor got that far because he said that Joe led him to some mountain where he could look down on a hidden lake, but there was no way of getting down to it."

"No way that Joe Quinn knew of, he meant."

"How far are we from the rattlesnakes now?" asked Tim.

"Just about far enough for our own good, and

you ain't going one foot further neither. Turn about." Sandy's tone gave no chance of any further argument, so they reluctantly followed his lead back along the trail to the mouth of the canyon. But Tim felt a good deal better. At least they had found the right canyon, and she knew about the black pine that was near the door, and they knew that the right trail led down from the top of the mountain to it, instead of up from the canyon where the snakes were. She made up her mind secretly that the next time she and Don went to hunt for it, they would leave Sandy behind, and start from the top of the mountain, but not a word did she breathe of this to either Don or Sandy on the way back.

" Seems like a person will have to satisfy their curiosity now by just looking up at the door," Sandy said placidly. " We'll make another trip over when we can stay a bit longer, and maybe I can locate it exactly for you, but you'll never climb to it till you grow wings."

Don stole a glance back at Tim, and Tim riding single file last of all on the trail, grinned back at him. They understood each other perfectly.

CHAPTER XV

For several days they discussed the best way of reaching the door by themselves. It would not do to leave it until summer, Don said, for two reasons, first of all Mother would be home and might not exactly approve of the exploration trip. Another thing, the weather would be altogether too hot by then. Even now it was unpleasant crossing the desert in the middle of the day. They would have to start around five in the morning, or even earlier.

"The best thing for us to do," he said, "is just to duck out quietly some Saturday, and instead of going anywhere near the Splinter, just cut straight across to the Horseshoe. We can find the right mountain now since we've found out it's only two from Dave's place on Lookout. Locate Lookout, and count two peaks back, and you've got the right one."

"I'd rather do just as Sandy told us to, Don, and start from the Splinter. He's been an old scout and he knows the best thing to do. We'll

come to the canyon that he took us up. I'll know
it the minute I see it, know how? There's a big
cactus right where you go in."

"We won't go in, though. We're going to try
it from the top this time, locate the black pine,
and work down from that point."

Tim listened, but did no more arguing. She
was too busy thinking, trying to remember
whether or not the place where they had found
Pablo and Pinto the day of the forest fire was
not on a mesa between Lookout and this other
mountain east. The trouble was that only Lookout had any name. All the other mountains in
the Horseshoe looked so much alike that it was
hard to tell them apart. You just had to watch
the difference in their skyline shape, and remember that the canyon mouths were all different
too. Some were narrow and winding and lost
to view almost as soon as they left the edge of the
desert, and others were, as Dave said, wide and
handsome, with plenty of space and beauty of
scenery like Lookout Canyon.

"What's the matter?" asked Don.

"Nothing, I was only thinking about Pablo
and the day we found him, remember? I just

feel that he knows a lot he never tells. If we talked to him and told him what Sandy told us, maybe he'd lead us straight to the door. He goes away and explores every place you can think of, Don, Indian fashion. He must know."

"I shouldn't wonder," Don returned very sarcastically. "Don't you want to invite a few more and make it a week-end picnic? You're never satisfied to go along with me alone."

"Oh, it isn't that at all, Don," protested Tim earnestly. "I do believe in you, but you take so long to do anything. You have to think about it and plan, and I'd like to go this Saturday."

"Can't. I promised Dick Thorpe I'd take him out hunting rabbits, and Sandy's loaning us Powder. Dick wouldn't like any girls along. You know how he is, English."

"He isn't when you know him. It's just you, yourself, Don, and you're trying to put it off on Dick. You don't want me to go. Here I am, all waiting to go on our trip and you make a date to shoot bunnies and gophers with Dick."

"He's going away pretty soon, that's why."

"Who told you that? Margot never said one word to me about it, and I don't believe it."

"Dick told me, and so did Sam come to think of it, so it's town news by now." Don whistled softly as he purposely delayed telling all that he knew. It was a novelty for him to get hold of any news before Tim. "I heard that Mr. Thorpe's going back to New York. Father heard that too, down in Oro."

"Why? I thought he came here to do some good?"

"Maybe he meant to, but he's found out there isn't anything here,—no gold, silver, oil,—just nothing. We're all dead and don't know it, that's all."

Tim stared at him in flat disapproval and unbelief. "Why, he hasn't been here long enough to find out anything, Don. He hasn't really hunted around, or had drill tests made, you know that. He's just peeked here and there. I don't believe what he says. Oh, but wouldn't it be wonderful if after he's gone, we found out there was gold up the canyon just as Sandy says there is."

"Plenty much-a," grinned Don, "plenty much-a gold."

"Well, laugh if you want to; you saw the nugget just the same as I did, and it was certainly gold. Don't you even believe Sandy?"

Don merely whistled, and applied himself more closely than ever to polishing the deep russet tan of his saddle leather to a high lustre. Tim waited impatiently, and he sang at her a refrain from one of Tom's cowboy range songs:

" Oh, if ever I ride that way again,
        You may call me absolute' insane."

" Oh, very well, be superior and silly, if you want to," Tim said haughtily. "I have every idea that you'll leave me out as usual and you'll go over there with Sandy some day, and find the door all by yourself. If you try it, I just hope you'll slip and slide on a toboggan all the way down the mountain."

" Sweet l'il sister," called Don after her. " Nice-a baby pineapple." But Tim walked up to the house and did not even glance back. It was quite evident to her that Don, her special comrade among the McLeans, was preferring boys to herself on his desert jaunts, and it made her furious just to think of it.

When she got in her own room, she looked at

herself in the mirror. It was a very large one,
but by standing on a chair she could manage to
get a fairly good view of Katherine Campbell,
and the longer she looked at her, the more she
disapproved of her general get-up. Old tan
corduroy riding pants of Don's, high calfskin hiking boots just like the boys wore, and an old
pongee shirt without a tie, and one of Neil's old
belts. It was about time, she thought, that she
gave the matter of clothes some attention.

Margot did not come out to the ranch with
Dick on Saturday, so Tim decided to ride in and
visit her, and ask her if it was really true that the
Thorpes were leaving Frisbee. It seemed as if
the Garden House was the only cool spot in town
as she left Chapo in the side drive, and went
through the garden to the house. Tumpy was
happily sleeping in the couch hammock when she
passed by, and Tim just opened the front screen
door and whistled softly. After a minute or so
Margot's head appeared over the upper stairway
as she leaned over to see who it was.

"Just me," Tim said. "Can I come up?"

"Oh, do, I'm packing, and I've got many more
things than I know what on earth to do with."

"Then you are going," Tim accused. "I didn't believe it when Don told me."

"We must because Father's all through here, and we're going to New York and then to London. Tumpy hates crossing the ocean. She's always terribly ill, and that gives Dick and me a chance to run over the whole ship, so all she does is lie and worry for fear we'll take a header into the deep and briny any minute."

Tim flung her cap far from her, and sat down on the couch. "I wouldn't like any old Tumpy keeping an eye on me after I was thirteen."

"But Tumpy thinks we're all just children, and she's a sweet old thing after all. We're going to visit my grandmother down in Kent. Oh, and Tim, I wish you could see her home there, it's wonderful."

"Castle, ivy covered?" Tim inquired listlessly. She felt warm and tired after her rapid ride in from the mesa.

"It is ivy covered, but it's an old country house, they call it Mobley Towers, and it's haunted and everything."

"If you don't keep still you'll find me in your suitcase," Tim warned. "I'd rather travel than do anything else in the world. Why do you have to go away so soon? Your father hasn't half looked around Frisbee. Doesn't he think there's any kind of ore around here?"

"He hasn't said anything to me about it," Margot answered. "He only looks places over and makes a report on them for his company back in New York."

"I know, but how can he be sure unless he makes all sorts of drill tests, or whatever they do?"

"But they don't hunt for gold the way they used to, Tim. I mean just dig for it. They locate the drifts on the geological survey charts, I think, just as they do with copper, and somehow they can tell where the veins pass through. Maybe I'm all wrong. Dick is much cleverer than I am, but I think they decide from the charts and calculations."

"Doesn't sound one bit like gold mining to me," Tim said. "Maybe he's hunting oil, but then, they have to drill for oil too. I'll bet a nickel some day they'll hunt for ore with an airplane. And it will have some sort of magic ray attached to it like a search-light, only it will penetrate the ground and show where there is ore. I'd like to patent that idea."

They both laughed, and then forgot all about gold strikes. Margot got out her three books full of snapshots she had taken in England and all around on her travels with her father, and they looked at these for a while before deciding it would be more fun to slip past Tumpy and go down town after marshmallow sundaes and mail.

Tim had half forgotten what Margot had said until that night at dinner she happened to hear Mr. McLean tell Tom that the Thorpe decision was adverse, he had heard, so there was no chance of Frisbee facing another mining boom.

"What was he looking for, Father?" Tim asked.

"Well, he didn't go around telling people that, Tim. I'd say oil if he wasn't with the Hayes-Roberts group. They've been making drill tests, I've heard, all the way from here down to Oro."

"But the gold isn't that way," Tim exclaimed before she thought. "It's way over in the Horse-shoe." Here she caught Don's eyes fixed on her with a positively fierce expression of wrathful warning, and she subsided instantly.

"According to Sandy and Jim Quinn?" asked her father teasingly. "I guess the best claims always lay to the southwest and that's where they still think they'll strike it again. It's too bad in a way, because if Thorpe had given us a good report, we'd have a railroad through here."

"Why did you and Mother ever build a home here instead of going down to Oro when everybody else went?" asked Tom.

"There were reasons; first she liked it here best, and it was our first home in the west. Another thing, she always believed the strike would come again."

"So do I," Tim said positively.

"I'll bet anything Mother wishes she were back home this minute," Neil said while munching an ear of corn. Tim looked at his hands.

"Maybe you'll wash your hands before you come to the table if she does come home."

"That's only automobile paint, smarty," flashed back Neil with hurt indignation. "Powder stuck his nose in a can that was half full and it stuck, and I had to get him out."

"What's Powder doing way over here? I didn't see Sandy around to-day."

"He just ran away by himself, Tim, so let him alone, will you? He got his nose all chewed in a gopher hole and I'm taking care of him. Then I tried to get the paint off with turpentine and he nearly had a fit."

"So would you, if your nose was raw in spots. It's a wonder you didn't put on gasoline as a happy thought."

"Now, listen here, boss," Tom put in, "you can pick on me all you like because I can handle you, but not on little Neil. Just because you happen to be the only female in the family is no reason for you to tease and bully the rest of us, eh, Dad?"

Before Tim realized what was going to happen to her, Tom picked her up bodily in his arms and carried her out to the couch hammock and dumped her unceremoniously among the cushions. "Will you promise to quit bossing?" he asked, and Tim struggled without giving up. Estrella watched the fight from behind the kitchen screen door, but Tim did not appeal for help. She fought like a little wildcat, and Tom finally swung her over his shoulder and carried her to the patio pool.

"In you go if you don't promise quick," he said, and hanging head downward over the water puppies and frogs and lizards Tim still vowed she would never say she was sorry. Tom promptly lowered her down until her head touched the pool and her hair got all wet, but Tim screwed her face up and shut her eyes and dared him to drop her in.

"Then promise to let Neil alone when he doesn't wash his hands." Tim finally promised this much, and Tom set her on her feet with her hair plastered in a drippy fringe over her eyes, and these same eyes glaring at him stormily.

"Just because you happen to be nineteen, any-body'd think you were Napoleon Jr.," she flung after him as a last shot, then she decided she wouldn't join the family circle at all. She would shut herself up in her own room, and write a long letter to her mother. Not that she really told on the boys in it, but she did try to convey the idea that she thought it might be a good thing if Mrs. McLean would come home soon and make the boys behave themselves.

She sat back after she had written the letter and felt lonely because the boys did not come and

beg her to come out and join them. She wished
she had a sister like Margot, then life would have
been much happier and easier, an elder sister
about fifteen. She knew that she was going to
miss Margot terribly, just as they were getting
really friendly so that they felt acquainted, it
seemed all wrong for her to go away to England.
Of course there were lots of other girls in the
school at Frisbee, but none of them just suited
Tim as a close friend. She, herself, was imagina-
tive and romantic and loved adventure quite as
much as a boy did, and Margot had a valiant
streak in her that Tim admired since the day of
the fire. She was cool headed and fearless in
danger, and she loved books and travel. Tim
instinctively admired her, and was interested in
the stories she could tell of the strange places and
people she had seen. Margot had promised faith-
fully she would write often, and perhaps some
time Mr. Thorpe might be sent out to the Southwest again and they would see each other. But
then again, she had also said that their grandmother wanted them both to stay in England and
go to school.

" Oh, dear," Tim thought desolately as she

curled up on the wide seat by the narrow window that looked toward the mountains, " there's always someone in every family who plays policeman and makes everyone else behave. In our family it's Tom because Father and Mother aren't one bit that way." The rebellious tears rose slowly to her lashes and fell down on her hands clasped under her chin. She wondered who Tom got his aggravating ways from and remembered suddenly that she had heard he was like the Powell side of the family, Grandma and Grandpa Powell who lived up above Buffalo, on Grand Island, a fascinating place that Tim had always longed to visit. Her mother had remarked that she might bring Grandma Powell back with her if she could only persuade her to take the long trip. Tim wondered uneasily just what grandmothers did when they took their rightful places in families, sort of old queen dowagers probably. She saw in imagination a very indignant, stout old white haired lady who would say firmly, " Katherine Campbell McLean, you mind your mother instantly when she speaks to you." Mother wasn't one bit that way, Tim thought mournfully, and she leaned her head now on the window sill and cried. Mother was lovely and understanding, even if she did spoil them.

She felt ever so much better after a good cry, and read her letter all over again. "When are you ever coming home?" it said. "I simply can't stand this life without you any longer. Estrella bosses me, and Tom thinks he is my special keeper. I'd rather live with Sandy and the burros than stay here, and I wish you'd come back home soon, please."

Somehow it sounded like a dreadful bleat now. Tim looked at it doubtfully. It might worry her mother and make her start home too soon, so after meditating a minute, she tore up the letter and sat down to write another, full of the interesting things she was doing, and all about Margot, and the forest fire, without one word to trouble her mother's mind. The ranch was going along splendidly, Estrella was an old darling, and the boys were behaving themselves. Then in large printed letters she wrote:

"AND SO AM I.
Your loving daughter,
TIMMIE."

CHAPTER XVI

THE next day marked the beginning of new
resolutions put into active execution for Tim.
From now on until her mother returned, she
made up her mind absolutely that she would behave herself, and that meant no more long rides
into the desert out to Sandy's, and no more wild
jaunts up into the mountains hunting, as Neil
said, " things that ain't." She would be a real
girl like Margot and stop racing around after
Don and making believe that she was his twin
brother.

The first act of self-sacrifice was to take her
old hiking boots and the corduroy pants and roll
them all up together and pitch them into a far
corner of her clothes closet. Next, she decided
that she would dress like Margot in pretty, ruf-
fly, light dresses. But after she had spent an
hour digging resolutely into bureaus, trunks,
chests, and closets, she found only three worth
while; her very best white dress, and two linen
smocks, one linen skirt and two blouses. The

smocks had been tan and pink, but were faded now and so was the skirt. They did not make a good showing at all for a person who proposed transforming herself from a ranch tomboy into a proper Junior High School girl. She stuffed all the dresses back into the closet and went out to find her father and talk things over with him.

He sat out on the veranda after supper, reading a magazine and smoking. He looked mighty comfortable, but Tim perched herself on the arm of his chair, and turned his face toward her firmly.

"Listen, Douglas McLean," she said earnestly, "I have something terribly important to say to you. First of all, do you love me?"

Mr. McLean laughed and swept her down into his lap to be properly assured. "Now then, what do you want, Timmie?" he asked. "And don't be all night about it because I want to read while there's daylight."

Timmie pressed a vague kiss on the side of his head.

"You happen to be the father of Katherine Campbell McLean, see? All right, then listen to her. She's tired of wearing boys' pants."

She watched the effect solemnly. Mr. Mc-Lean's eyes twinkled but he kept his face sober, only that his mouth would pucker a little as if he were trying hard not to laugh.

" No boys' pants," he repeated, " then what? "

Tim's hands swept a large circle in the air, " Dresses, much-a. I must have some, with ruffles, pretty girl ones. I've even been wearing corduroy pants to school when I rode over. Oh, I know lots of the girls wear them to ride in, but it's just a habit, Father, and I think if I make myself wear decent dresses like Margot, maybe I'll stop wanting to go chasing off to Sandy's or up in the mountains or hunting rabbits or playing all the time with Don."

" It's an idea," agreed her father, " but suppose you go fifty-fifty, wear dresses half the time and corduroys the other half."

" They're too hot anyway. I've got some of Don's old linen and khaki ones," Tim said gloomily.

" But we wouldn't know what to make of you if you spring this change on us all at once. Hadn't you better wait until your mother comes home? "

"Certainly not," Tim declared flatly. "That's another reason why I just must start in to train myself so I'll be different when she gets home. She might bring Grandma Powell with her, and can you imagine what a shock it would be for her to get her first glimpse of her one and only granddaughter looking like a tramp cowboy? I thought this thing all out last night with tears and sobs and everything, and I believe the boys would treat me better if I dressed up and stopped being —well, on such familiar terms with them. Don't you dare laugh at me," as he started to, "or I'll never speak to you again on a serious subject like this. Truly, Father, I mean it, this is a very important crisis."

"How much do you need?" he asked.

Tim thought hard, but couldn't figure it out. "I'm not sure, but I thought I'd get Margot Thorpe to go with me because she knows the right things to buy. They haven't a thing around here in Frisbee, so do you mind if I drive down to Oro with her to buy what I need? She'll probably drag Tumpy along to take care of us. Just give me twenty dollars and I'll bring back the change."

" Better make it twenty-five. You'll need new shoes too and before you get through, you'll want a new hat. I know these women when they get their hearts set on new clothes." Mr. McLean counted out two tens and a five and handed them to Tim. She took them in her hands and folded them up very small, her face flushed and self-conscious. Then she looked him squarely in the eye. " I'll never forget this, Father," she said, trying to be very serious, but all at once they laughed together, and Tim felt a lot easier. " I guess," she added confidentially, as she hugged him closely, " that maybe I just wanted to surprise Mother and Grandmother even more than the boys."

" I guess it isn't anything only you're growing up. Come and get more if you should need any." He patted her cheek and Tim went away with the money fairly clutched in one happy fist. What she wouldn't do with twenty-five dollars. Dazzle the boys first of all. She only wanted to see the expression on Tom and Don's faces when they caught the first glimpse of her. She did not even let Estrella know what she was going to do when she left the ranch early the next day.

Don fulfilled his threat and rode off early into the desert with Dick and some of Don's friends and Neil. But Tim did not make any protest, nor even appear to notice what they were doing. She stayed in her own room until they had disappeared down the canyon trail, then she came out and slipped down to get the car out without Estrella seeing her. She wore her tan linen sport skirt and one of the white blouses. Although they were old, they showed her intentions.

Margot fell in with the plan at once, but Tumpy had to be convinced of the importance of immediately getting Chester out to drive the girls down to Oro.

"It is vairee hot," she protested. "I do not zink it at all imperative that it happen to-day."

"But Tumpy dear, can't you understand?" Margot spoke carefully. "Mademoiselle Tim wishes to have the new dress, look at me, Tumpy," and she pointed to her own rows of frocks hanging in the long wardrobe against the wall, "ze robe *jeune fille, n'est-ce pas?*"

Tumpy caught the idea perfectly now, and smiled and nodded at Tim, as she ran off a long string of French at her.

"Certainly," said Tim cordially. "What did she tell me, Margot?"

Margot translated laughingly, and added that Tumpy thought she needed stockings too, silk ones. They drove down thirty miles to Oro and found several fairly good shops along the main street. It was Margot's first visit, and she said it was like a little model of any middle western small town except for the new Spanish stucco depot with the bright red tile roof.

"Well, I suppose so many people come out here from the middle west, that they try to make it look as much like home as possible," Tim said. "You see, Frisbee started out with the general idea of just what it wanted to be, and it built itself around the plaza and the little mission church, but Oro never even wanted to be artistic. It's just a mining town, all business places and the Grand Central Hotel, and nobody lives down here who doesn't have to."

Nevertheless, Margot said the New York styles were right there in Oro, and they found what they were looking for in two sport dresses, a pair of tan strap sandals with higher heels than Tim had ever had on walking shoes, and a sport hat that gave her, as she herself said, a very nifty appearance.

"I don't believe even the burros would know me in this," she pulled the rakish little soft felt lower on one side, and decided she would wear one of the dresses back home, the green and tan wash silk that matched her curious eyes and her own coat of tan. Also the sandals of woven tan leather.

"Ah, *mais oui,*" exclaimed Tumpy, clapping her hands together when she saw the effect from the car window, and at the demonstration, several leading citizens, as Tim said later on, stopped to look at the effect. "*C'est tres chic!*"

"Like it, Chester?" Tim asked as she climbed in the car hastily to escape further scrutiny. Chester turned his head with dignity and surveyed the ensemble.

"I should say, miss, that it would be very hard to beat."

"Then drive on, for pity's sake." Tim sank back with relief on the deeply cushioned seat, while Margot laughed. "Well, I only hope it strikes the McLean outfit the same way," Tim surveyed herself in the mirror ahead of her, and frowned doubtfully. " It's nice of course, but somehow, Margot, it doesn't seem to be me at all. I think I've gone and done it this time good and plenty, and when we get to your place, I'm going to take it all off, and put on my old clothes so as to spring it on the boys by easy degrees."

Accordingly when she reached the ranch at six o'clock, there was nothing at all in her appearance to satisfy the curious, except that she seemed to give special care to a certain strange suitcase, and hustled it out of sight into the closet in her room.

At the dinner table her father gave her a quizzical look and Tim smiled back at him beamingly and nodded her head. Don caught her doing it, and looked at her suspiciously.

"' Just what have you been up to all day? "

" My own personal affairs, eat your dinner in peace, darling," retorted Tim severely. " How many little bunnies got away to-day? "

Never was Tim so impossible and aggravating to her brothers as when she chose to take this calm and superior tone with them, or as Don said, high-hat them. To-night she was worse than ever with the comforting memory of the new

dresses and shoes and hat to make her feel that
she had really cut loose from all tomboy ways
forever. She listened with a bored and far-away
expression to Neil and Don's vivid description
of the rabbit hunt, and how Dick tried to get a
coyote but it got away. Tim's eyelids lowered.

"Naturally it would," she said.

"Say, what on earth ails you?" Don demanded. "You know you're not Deadshot Dick
yourself by any means."

"My ambitions do not run that way," said
Tim very sweetly. "Excuse me, Father, please."
The boys all watched her as she left the room,
and Tom rubbed his head vigorously.

"What's up, I wonder, do you know,
Father?"

Mr. McLean glanced at Tim's disappearing
form out in the patio and smiled mysteriously.
"Women folks are very peculiar and hard to
understand," he said. "I guess Tim's just all
girl like the rest of them."

"Well, she doesn't have to show off with us,
does she?" Don protested. "She's thinking up
something, I know her, to get even with us, but
it wasn't our fault. Dick never likes to go hunt-

ing with girls, he says. I thought Tim would go
with Margot."

"Guess she did, didn't she?"

"I don't know, she acts awfully funny and
queer to me." Don gave it up and followed Neil
down to their favorite corner near the corral
where they had a new family of baby owls in a
eucalyptus tree.

Tim paid no attention to any of them, but shut
herself in her room and tried on both dresses, the
green and tan, and a pink and white sport silk
with a pink suede belt and no sleeves. Her hair
looked wrong and she tried one effect after the
other, finally parting it on one side to try and
make it look wind-blown like Margot's. This was
hard since Tim's own curly brown hair came to
her shoulders, but maybe she would have it cut
off, she thought.

After a while she stepped out into the moonlit
patio and listened. Someone was playing on a
mandolin under the pepper trees, probably
Pablo, and the boys were there too because she
heard their voices. So she tiptoed softly across
the tiled court and into the living-room where her
father sat at his desk.

" Rather. She looks best when she's in the saddle anyway, no frills for Tim, they just don't go with her."

Later in the day Tim might have agreed with him. She stood the frills until around four and then changed into her riding outfit and mounted Chapo in desperation for a good gallop to wear off the effects of the day. But she went alone, determined not to give in to the boys or associate with them. They could keep right to themselves, she thought. She would never try to manage or help them again, she got no thanks for it. They just called her a boss, and Tim was through with brothers.

But the next morning she wakened with a start, feeling somehow that it was late for school, and sure enough, when she looked the little round clock on the table near her bed said nine twenty-two. She was out of bed in a second and dashed to the door.

" Estrella! " she called. " What's the matter? Why didn't you call me? "

" All right, all right," came Estrella's soothing voice. " The papa say you rest, too much ride, too tired."

"Oh, bother," Tim exclaimed throwing her clothes every which way as she hunted for stockings. Finally she found an old pair of Chinese slippers and put them on her bare feet, with a faded blue kimono over her pajamas. A good wash in cold water and a vigorous brushing of her hair and she appeared glowing, for breakfast. Estrella set an appetizing tray down beside her, grape fruit, cocoa, and Tim's favorite Spanish omelet. And last of all a spray of lemon blossoms.

"You're a blessing to me, after all, Estrella," Tim sighed, as she consented to curl up on the couch and enjoy breakfast. "Why didn't those demon brothers of mine call me for school?"

"The papa say no, much-a rest, good baby sleep."

"I'm not going to rest when there's nothing the matter with me," Tim answered flatly. "I wish I could get Margot over for the day. Where's Pablo? I'll send him after her."

Estrella wrinkled up her face, closed her eyes, shook her head with upraised eyes and signified that she had no idea where Pablo might be. Tim looked at her suspiciously. "That means he's surely up to something, and you won't tell. More snakes, I wonder?"

"No snake," Estrella protested fervently. "He go Sandy way off."

"He did? What for?" Tim's eyes stared with new interest. "Where did he go with Sandy, tell me?"

But Estrella merely shrugged her ample shoulders, picked up the tray and moved along easily. Tim's first impulse was to get Chapo and ride over to Sandy's by herself to find out what was going on between him and Pablo, but this new pose of grown-upness interfered with such a move. It was lonesome too around the ranch without the boys, she found out as the morning wore on. She never had realized how still it was way up on the mesa with the sleepy little ranch lying half hidden under the big pepper and eucalyptus trees.

Finally after wandering around by herself to look at the puppies and the ponies, and all the other pets of the ranch, Tim took a book to read and climbed up in the big olive tree where long ago Tom had built a tree house for the children. Pieces of board nailed to the long sloping trunk made a good ladder, and Tim went up it like a cat and perched herself in the little enclosed platform that was hidden from view to anyone down below. The book proved more interesting than she had expected, one of Don's about head hunters in New Guinea, and she was soon deeply absorbed in it. Time passed until it was noon and Estrella stuck her head out of the kitchen door and called Tim's name shrilly. But Tim read on. Serves her right, she thought, for not telling where Pablo went with Sandy. Anyway, she wasn't really hungry because she had such a late breakfast and she wanted to find out whether the band of explorers escaped from the head hunters and reached the hidden Valley of Gold.

All at once from somewhere far out of sight up in the sky there came the unmistakable throb of a motor. Tim dropped her book instantly and sat up, listening. It must be Bob Darnton, the mail pilot. She hardly ever had a chance to see him pass over the mesa except on Saturdays. Scrambling down from the tree, she ran toward the landing field, looking up eagerly to see where the plane was. She could hear it plainly, but there was no sign of it yet. It was not a clear day. The air was hazy with light banks of white cloud, and when the big plane suddenly swung up from the southwest, it did not seem to be driving as it usually did, straight ahead, sure and direct in its flight as a migrating bird.

Tim watched it anxiously, wondering what Bob was trying to do. It was as if he was trying out some new kind of flying stunts. The plane dove this way and that, banking from side to side as it slowly descended, then it seemed to poise and waver uncertainly, and again regaining its balance, it dove earthward, swerving back and forth in long sweeping glides. Something was certainly wrong, and Tim felt alarmed, but did not know what to do. One thing was sure, he was trying to make a landing on the mesa, and she felt glad of that, but suddenly the noise of the pounding motor stopped altogether, and Tim knew the peril he was in.

Estrella came running from the house, waving her apron in the air and making anguished cries of fear, but Tim stood still, her hands clasped tightly on her breast, her face very tense and white. If only he would make the field and not

strike off over the edge of the canyon, or land
some place on the steep rocky mountainside back
of the mesa. She called up to him as if he could
hear her, but Estrella had dropped to her knees
and was saying her prayers breathlessly. Tim
ran forward following the direction the plane
seemed to be taking. It was on its last glide now,
over the yawning canyon, driving irresistibly, it
seemed, straight for the rocks hundreds of feet
below, when all at once it leaned sideways as if
one wing were broken, and swung over the mesa
just in time, as it struck.

Tim raced to where it lay like a great crumpled
bird with a broken wing. It seemed as if one
wing had been driven into the ground, but when
she reached the plane she saw the figure of the
pilot. He was trying to pull himself up out of
the wreck.

"Oh, are you hurt any?" she called to him.

"Don't know yet." He succeeded in freeing
himself and dragged his left leg out with a final
effort, his face screwed up hard. Then he swung
down to the ground and surveyed the plane.
"Gee, she got a rotten tumble, didn't she? I
tried to make the field, but the engine died on

me and I had to bank down at the last to make it at all."

" Well," Tim swallowed hard and tried to look cheerful. " It's a good thing the field was here, wasn't it? "

He turned his head and looked down at her as if he just realized she was there. " You bet it is," he replied fervently, and grinned. " Are you one of the McLeans? "

" Yes, I'm the girl—I mean I'm Tim McLean. My brother Don and I thought it up and planned it and he got a lot of his boy friends from school to help. We thought it would be a good idea to have a field here."

" Good thing for me you did or I might be a nice new grease spot over there on the wall of the canyon. Have you got anybody at the ranch who could help me get the mail sacks out? I've got to haul them to the nearest post office and get them off on the next train north."

" I can take you down," Tim said instantly, " and Estrella and I'll help you get the sacks out. I can drive the car, and Frisbee's only two miles away. But we haven't any trains out of there. Oro's the nearest station, thirty miles down."

" Then we go to Oro," Bob said positively. He started to climb up on the plane and Tim saw the muscles of his face tighten in quick pain.

" Didn't you get hurt, honestly? " she asked.

" Sure I did, jammed my leg. Stand by now, I'm going to drop the sacks out."

Estrella hurried up to help, joyous and thankful over his being alive, and between them, they helped him get the mail sacks out of the plane. Tim had never felt so important in all her life. In the first place the field had worked, it had done all they had hoped it might. Just to look at the plane as it lay there, one sided on the cleared ground, made her want to rub her eyes and make sure it was not a dream. The boys would be wild with envy when they found out what had happened while they were away. And she liked Bob Darnton. He was young and tall, with keen brown eyes and sandy, short clipped hair, and freckles, and his smile was wonderful. It was the cheeriest sort of a close lipped grin that took you at once into his confidence.

When the sacks were all safely out, Tim suggested that she go back to the ranch and drive the car over to the landing field where it would be easy to load. Estrella was concerned over Bob because he limped, but he refused to bother over his own injury; the important thing was to get the mail through. Tim drove the car when they got it safely loaded, and sat with Bob in the front seat. Never had she felt so thrilled, and she even forgot that she had on her usual ranch costume, old khaki riding pants, pongee shirt, and boots. She had put them on from habit when she dressed and now she had to ride beside her hero into Oro dressed like this instead of in one of her new outfits. But Tim hardly gave it a thought. She was anxious to get the mail through, as Bob wished.

When the old car rattled through Frisbee's main street, people stared after it in curious surprise to see a stranger in flying togs sitting beside Tim McLean, but Tim kept right on until she came to Sam's.

" We can find out here," she told Bob, " here comes our postmaster and I'll introduce you."

Sam came down the steps of the store staring at the load of mail sacks on the rear of the car.

" First aid to Uncle Sam, eh, Tim? " he said, but Tim wasted no time joking.

" This is Bob Darnton, mail pilot, and he fell on our field, so we're on our way down to Oro. When's the next train north, Sam? "

" Tell you pronto," Sam took the steps at one springing leap and dashed back in a few seconds. " Five eleven, no, that one only goes as far as Central Springs. Here's the right one, three-nineteen, express north to San Francisco, there you are. Why didn't you send us word so we could all come and help? "

" Didn't have time," grinned Bob. " And Tim here was giving me orders."

Sam smiled at Tim proudly. " Well, you sure did some good work making that field, Tim. Why ain't you in school where you belong Monday? "

" Can I use your 'phone? Got to report forced landing." Bob went on into the store followed by all the curious crowd of usual loungers around Sam's store.

" You're the nosiest thing I ever saw, Sam," Tim scolded. " What did you have to say that for in front of him? It's mighty lucky that I did stay home." She stopped short, her ears strained as she heard Bob talking on the telephone. His

voice reached her clearly, " Report forced landing on McLean's Field, two miles north of Frisbee. Mail O. K. Sending on 3:19 express out
of Oro."

There was plenty more, but Tim did not hear
it. She looked around at the group that hung
back from the car, Jim Quinn and all the others,
and back again to Sam's grinning, glowing face.
McLean's Field. Officially reported as such.
Tim felt a funny tingling all over, and she
wanted to suddenly laugh and cry too. But Bob
came hurrying out of the store, and she hastened
to start up the car. Of course of all times, it had
to buck and stall and cut up all of its usual
tricks, right before everybody. Jim pushed forward eagerly.

" I've got a good car if you want me to drive
you down to Oro," he said. Bob shook his head,
and climbed in beside Tim.

" This one's fine, thanks." And just as if it
appreciated the compliment, the old car made
up its mind to behave and started off down the
street, picking up speed good and proper to make
Oro in time for the 3:19.

CHAPTER XVIII

When the boys came home from school and found out what had happened, they both declared disgustedly it was just Tim's luck to be at the ranch the very day the plane fell. They had heard of the accident over in Frisbee as soon as they left school. Everyone was talking about how the big mail plane had taken a tumble over on the McLeans' landing field, and it was almost as if people felt Timmie had made good her announcement that the town needed one.

Then, as if all this were not enough, the boys had heard that Tim had taken Bob Darnton and the mail down to Oro in the old car. Even as late as four-thirty they had not returned, and the mesa back of the ranch was dotted with cars and sightseers who had come out to take a look at the wrecked plane. It was really the greatest excitement the little town had known since the gold fever. The Thorpes drove over and even Chester displayed a mild interest, and Mademoiselle wept with emotion over what might have happened. Jim Quinn strolled around giving advice on just how the plane could be restored until Sam asked him why he didn't call up Uncle Sam personally and tell him just what he considered should be done.

Even Sandy appeared, on Cleo, very calm and collected except for his fiery old eyes deep set under grizzled fringy eyebrows, as Tim called them. "Lucky for that pilot those two kids took a notion to make this soft place for him to light on," he remarked. "Little farther over the edge and he'd be flying with real wings."

Finally the rickety little car came rumbling up the canyon road with Tim at the wheel and Bob Darnton beside her, and they were both laughing and chatting together as if they were well acquainted.

"For the love of cats, hurry up, the mayor and chief of police are over there waiting for you," Don greeted Tim. Tim ignored his irritation and introduced Bob as if she wouldn't have cared even had foreign potentates and national notables been awaiting their arrival. It annoyed the boys the way she smiled at them cheerfully, and drove straight by them over to the field.

"Well, I suppose we have to follow them," Neil said. "Isn't she snooty, though, just because she happened to be on the spot when he slid down? Girls make me tired somehow, they always think they know more than anybody else."

Don felt peevish too, but he stuck his hands deep in his pockets and walked over to the field where he found Sandy and that comforted him a little bit. It was not until most of the people had gone that he finally found Tim. She was with Margot, dusty and tired but happy.

"I've never been congratulated in my whole life before," she said with a sigh of relief. "I wish Dave Watson had been here too. Everybody else was, it seemed. Sandy liked it too, and I think he really deserved the credit because he was the first to tell us about Bob, and hang out a lantern for him. I took him over and introduced him to Bob and he said he often wondered what that lone light was down in the middle of the desert, and whether it was meant for him."

"I don't see how you managed to be home today," said Don.

"I didn't manage anything. I never even meant to stay home from school, I overslept and

Estrella didn't wake me up in time, and after breakfast I went over to the tree house to read and when the mail plane came along it sounded queer and I saw it was sort of coasting and making turns instead of going straight ahead. I just wish you could have seen Sam and Jim and the rest at the store when we drove up to telephone. They were just simply petrified. And when we got down to Oro, they took our pictures."

"Just born lucky, that's all," Don said. "You know you don't deserve it because you never did any more work on that field than us boys did."

"Didn't I drive the mail down to Oro in time to make the express? Didn't I keep my head in a great emergency?"

"Hail! Hail!" Don swept her a mock curtsy, and drew an imaginary halo around her head. "Ain't she just marvelous?"

"I don't care what you say, Don, you're only sorry it wasn't you." Tim turned around to face Dick's quizzical close-lipped smile and lifted left eyebrow. "Well, say it," she said.

Dick smiled teasingly, "Keep your temper, no public character can afford to lose it because they might be taking your picture."

" Oh, you're terrible, Dick," said Tim crossly. " Come on, Margot, I don't want to stay and listen to them any longer."

" Is Bob Darnton going to stay here at the ranch until they send another plane after him? " asked Don.

" I think he is, he was talking with Father. He's like a captain with a ship, he doesn't want to leave it behind, and he's hurt his leg somehow, in the crash. I tried to make him see a doctor at Oro, but he said he didn't have time."

" Is he going to sleep here to-night? " asked Neil eagerly.

" Oh, don't ask me a million questions now, Neil, I'm tired."

" Who's asking a million? I only wanted to know so I can ride over and tell the rest of the boys who haven't seen him, and they can come back and get a look at him."

" Why don't you charge admission, darling? " Tim asked. " Go over and help him, it's the best thing you can do." She linked her arm in Margot's, and they strolled back to the house together. " Just the same," she said, " Bob did tell me confidentially that he was mighty glad our field was there ready for him, because it would have been awfully rough landing on the mesa the way it was before we cleared it off for him. Maybe now the town will vote for a real landing field. Bob says there should be a good one in every town of fair size, and there will be, some day, just like a post office or a Union Depot."

"Father said he thought your idea was fine because Frisbee is the last town on the edge of the desert. I know he'd help too, if they started anything before we go away."

"When are you really going, Margot?"

"In about two weeks; don't let's even think about it."

"If he had only found out there was any chance at all for gold mining around here, you wouldn't have to go, would you?"

"Not so soon, probably, but sometime we must go to school in England—as soon as we get over Tumpy."

Tim wished she dared give her a hint of what Sandy had told Don and herself, just to let Mr. Thorpe know he was all wrong about thinking Frisbee was dead, but she had given Don her

word that she would absolutely not breathe a
thing to anyone about Sandy's secret. "Well, I
wish I could say something to make him change
his mind, and I probably could, but I can't
possibly."

Margot looked at her in surprise then laughed,
Tim's expression was so comical. "What do you
mean, Timmie?"

"Can't possibly tell. It's a secret, only you
tell your father this much, he hasn't looked in
the right place for gold out here, and I know it."

That night after everything around the ranch
had quieted down, Don was aroused from his first
good sleep by Tim shaking his shoulder. "Come
on outside, I want to talk to you," she whispered,
"don't wake up Neil."

"I'm sleepy, go way," said Don. "What's the
matter, got another plane down?"

"Don't be cross," Tim urged, "come on out.
Here, throw that around you." She tossed a
Navajo blanket over to him, and went out to
wait. Don rolled out of bed and wrapped the
blanket about him Indian fashion and stalked
out with blinking eyes and tousled hair.

"What do you want anyhow?" he asked.

" No fair waking a fellow up in the middle of the night."

" It's only a little past eleven, goose. Father's still in there talking to Bob. I must talk to you." She led the way from the house out to one of her favorite spots for council or meditation, a rock on the edge of the canyon. Here she perched, her hands clasped about her knees, looking for all the world in the moonlight like Sandy's coyote on top of the Splinter.

" Don, listen to me, we just can't wait any longer. Margot says they are going back to England in two weeks."

" What of it? "

" Don't you see, if we could find the door in the mountain, and it did turn out to be Sandy's lost Spirit mine, or even if we could drive out the rattlesnakes and pick up some gold nuggets the way he did, we'd prove there was real gold over there."

" How do you suppose we're going to drive out about ten thousand rattlers from Blind Canyon? "

Tim merely stared dreamily ahead to where the canyon widened to the north as it rose higher before dipping down to the desert. "I think we had better start around four Saturday morning," she announced with decision. "Enough's enough, Don, and I've waited until I'm getting all dancey and fidgety like Chapo when he's in the corral too long. Will you go or won't you? That's all, but just make up your mind."

"And you yanked me out of bed to tell me that," grumbled Don. "All right, I'll go. Take plenty to eat, things that won't spoil, because we may be out all night. We ought to have a pack mule or burro."

"I'd love to borrow Cleo, she's so intelligent, if there was any way of deceiving Sandy about why we wanted her."

"He'd guess right away. We can take enough along on the ponies. Have Estrella make up a lot of tortillas, they're easy to carry." Don yawned. "Can I go back to bed now?"

"What do you suppose we'll do," Tim asked in a whisper, "when we get right in front of the door; have you thought of that, Don?"

"Open it, I suppose, and we'd better take something along to help."

"But we can't drag a crowbar across the desert, Don, how about taking a hatchet, then you could chop it open if you have to. And ropes, two ropes good and long, in case we fall. They'd come in very handy if one of us fell off the edge of the canyon and landed on a ledge or in a tree."

"Say, what is this, a nightmare?" Don exclaimed aggrievedly. "It's going to be dangerous all right, but what's the use of cooking it all up to-night to worry over?"

"All right," Tim got up reluctantly. "I'll carry a blanket in case we do have to stay overnight. It's awfully cold way up in the mountains at night. I have a feeling that we ought to take something with us too, in case of rattlesnakes."

"Take Powder or Pablo, both are sure death to rattlers. Go to bed now, and stop talking to me, I'm sleepy. We'll start around five Saturday morning, and if you tell anyone I won't go at all."

Tim went back to her bed and undressed, but was far too excited to sleep. First she wished that she might go out on the mesa and see the plane. It would look so strange sprawled out like a great griffon, and it would be so thrilling to see it there at all instead of dangling over the rocky canyon somewhere in a crushed wreck.

Bob was still talking to her father and Tom, out on the narrow, vine-covered veranda that ran across the front of the ranch house. She could hear their voices as finally she fell asleep, her mind full of the coming trip and wondering whether Frisbee would really have a landing field some day.

The next day Bob and two mechanics worked on the plane with an interested audience standing by. Estrella was happy and excited over the stream of cars coming and going over the unfrequented old canyon road, and Tim begged hard to be allowed to stay home from school, but her father said no, a good sport did not cut exams to watch a plane being repaired, so she had to drive over with the boys in the morning. Still, when she did get to school she discovered that she was a local heroine for a day, and this was some compensation for having to plunge straight into a math. exam. when neither her heart nor mind would behave or pay attention.

The worst of it was that when they did reach home the plane had taken off and was gone from the mesa. Only one thing remained, Bob's cap, trampled and dusty as it had been kicked about underfoot by the sightseers around the plane, but Tim recognized it at once and pounced upon it as her own souvenir and trophy. She brushed it off carefully and hung it up in her room to remember her most thrilling hour by, not that she could ever forget it, but at least here was something tangible to remind her.

The next morning Pablo was down at the corral working around in his slow, easy-going way. Tim had decided she would ride over to school because she wanted to see if there was mail for her at Sam's afterwards, and while she saddled Chapo, she asked Pablo where he had been all day yesterday during the excitement.

" Mountains," Pablo replied vaguely.

" More snakes, I suppose. Where do you go for them, Pablo? Ever go way up Blind Canyon? "

Pablo shrugged his shoulders and backed into the barn after more feed.

" Most aggravating person I ever saw," Tim

flung after him as she mounted, and Chapo made his usual half circling, high stepping dash down the road. She had intended getting further information from Pablo about just where the snakes began up in the canyon. The day passed tiresomely, with Tim dreamy and sleepy too, looking out of the schoolroom window at the sky and wondering where Bob's plane was now. After school was out she did not stop to talk with anyone, but rode down to the post office to see if her usual letter was there from Buffalo.

"Well, you certainly did stir up something exciting, Tim," Sam remarked as he handed it out to her. "Understand the plane took off safely, couldn't have been much damaged after all."

"Everything inside was all right, it was just the left wing that got smashed, and they mended that." Tim was too busy trying to read her letter to go into details.

"Anything new up in Buffalo?" asked Sam with interest. "It's about time your mother was getting homesick for Frisbee, I'd say. Folks come out West, though, and they never lose that feeling for the East, not when they're born there.

I don't myself. Always plan to sell out and go back and look at the familiar spots of childhood. Remember that old oaken bucket song, Tim? Well, I want to tell you that the house where I was born in Rhode Island had that identical old oaken bucket dangling on the end of these long poles you let down into a well, and the bucket had moss on it too, and never in all my life East or West have I ever tasted such crystal clear cold water as came out of that homestead well."

" I never knew you were a real Yankee, Sam."

" You didn't eh? Well, I may have changed considerable after twenty-odd years of baking in this glorious sunlight, sort of dried up like a raisin, but I was born in Burrillville, and brought up over the state line in Putnam, Connecticut, and that's where old General Israel Putnam rode his horse up the steps of the capitol house."

" That was at Hartford, wasn't it, Sam? "

" Was it? Well, they named the town after him anyhow. Have some fig bars and a nibble of cheese? When's your mother coming home, does she say this time? "

" Next week—she's going to telegraph."

" Shucks, and they'll get the news first down

at the Western Union in Oro. Well, let me
know as soon as you can, Tim, I like news, you
know."

" I know," Tim laughed. " May I have a dill
pickle too, please? Where's the professor? I'd
like to say hello to him."

" Gone." Sam made a wide and comprehen-
sive gesture. " Took it in his head all at once to
clear out, and he made the stage yesterday afternoon, bound for Indiana. And not one single
authentic bone to take back with him as a prehistoric souvenir. I felt sorry for the old boy
'cause he had so much faith, and he was likable
too. He and Sandy have been swapping big
stories out there on the porch, seeing which could
go the other one better. I think the professor
came out ahead. But Sandy did tell him he had
a lump of pure gold big as a pigeon's egg that
came right out of the Horseshoe Range, and he'd
show it to him if he came by his shack. Believe it? "

" Not as big as a pigeon's egg," Tim said, then
she had to press her lips together tightly to keep
from saying all the things she wanted to as she
took the dill pickle from a big glass jar and said

good-bye. But she lost no time in riding back to the ranch to tell Don. Between the news of her mother arriving next week, and Sandy boasting of his nugget find on the Horseshoe, Tim felt that the sooner they found the door in the mountain, the better, before all the world started to follow Sandy up Blind Canyon after gold.

CHAPTER XIX

SATURDAY morning Don awakened first, around four-thirty, and slipped out of bed without disturbing Neil. Without knowing it, Neil had helped in the expedition because he had kept Powder at the ranch when he rambled over to visit his relatives. Don said the real reason why Powder liked to run away from Sandy's shack and visit the ranch was because he found plenty of bones, it was not any longing to see his brothers at all.

Estrella had willingly made a lot of delicious fresh tortillas for them, and surprised Timmie by putting in two chicken tamales too, because Tim always craved them on Saturdays. Two tin lunch boxes were packed and strapped to the backs of the saddles. Water they could probably find in the canyon, but to make sure Don took along Tom's old scout canteen, well filled, some matches, a hatchet and one rolled blanket that Tim insisted would come in handy if they had to stay out all night on the mountain. Last of all Don took along a good long rope coiled and hung in lariat fashion around his saddle horn, and a flashlight in his pocket. " You'd think the way we're fitting out that we expected to be gone a week," he grumbled when Tim suggested as a last happy thought, that they take along fish hooks and lines.

They rode down the canyon road just as day was breaking, and Tim heaved a sigh of relief. " You know, Don, I was thinking of one thing that we should do," she said. " Suppose anything did happen to us, oh, I know you'll say it's crazy to say that, but it might. Nobody knows where we're going, so they couldn't come after us if we did get lost."

" A girl would think of that," Don replied. " What do you want me to do, post up signs all the way over to Blind Canyon? We're not going into any kind of danger, just get that right out of your mind. We'll only ride over and try the other side of the mountain to see if there is a trail down to the big pine."

" I won't say another single word, but I'm telling you it's plain common sense to do it."

" I've managed everything, so don't you worry.

Nothing's going to happen, but if you don't stop grouching all the way, something will happen. You'll turn right around and go back home."

"Well, I like that, Donald McLean, when it's just as much my idea as it is yours. I would not turn back, I can tell you that right now. I am going on this time no matter what you say or do. Sandy'll put that nugget on exhibition in Benito's window if we don't look out, he's so proud of knowing something about where it came from, he just can't resist telling people about it."

"All right, don't get angry now and fussy at the start. I didn't eat any breakfast, did you?"

"Certainly, I found a melon and some crackers. We'll stop as soon as we get down to the desert and eat if you want to, Don."

But Don said he'd rather wait until they were across the desert and Tim told him if he was bound and determined to be heroic and suffer to go right ahead. She rode behind him all the way down the road until it started up grade again and looped about to the top of the ridge above the canyon.

Here they rested to see the sunrise. The light broke in great waves of radiance, first deep violet shot with pearl and rose, and last of all a glory of gold that seemed to flood the world. Here Don relented enough in the keen air to open up his lunch and eat something, then they descended the last trail to the desert. Here in spite of the extra burdens, the ponies freshened up after their long cautious trip and dashed off for a good race over the level land.

Don had said they would not go to the Splinter to wait until noon for Sandy's shadow to give them the right line to the mountain. He was certain he could find it now; it was the second peak east of Lookout. Even Tim felt confident about this, and that she herself remembered all the landmarks around the mouth of Blind Canyon. Powder raced along after them, delighted and surprised to find himself a member of this unexpected party. He chased young rabbits and one big jackrabbit that leaped ahead of him like a baby kangaroo, Tim said, and set all the gophers into a panic by dashing at them as they were peacefully sitting out in front of their ground burrows.

They reached the mountains around ten-thirty, tired and hungry, and found a cool spot to camp a little way up the canyon. Tim thought they'd better eat the tamales first, and some of Estrella's walnut cake, then they lay on their backs resting, their arms clasped beneath their heads while Powder dozed near the ponies.

"Where do you think you'll leave Chapo and Dusty?" Tim asked. "They can't go so very far after we leave the trail."

"Go as far as we can for that matter and better too, probably, but they can stay behind any place that looks as if they could get any grass to munch at while we're gone. We'll go as far as we can on them and then on foot, and we'd better start going."

"We can rest a while, Don, I'm tired." Tim wished she might take a nap like Powder. He looked so comfortable all stretched out flat and limp like a rag dog.

"I thought you'd be, just when we were about half-way here." Don got no farther because Tim was right on her feet and after Chapo indignantly. She didn't see why it was that Don and she quarrelled lately, they never used to, but now it seemed as if he tried to make her feel she was just a girl, instead of his pal as she had always

been.   Maybe he was jealous of Margot and her
friendship, Tim thought, and this made her
tolerant because she knew she had been giving
the Garden House a good deal of her society
lately.

Don took the trail over the east side of the
mountain where they might be able to look down
on Blind Canyon and locate the black pine.   Tim
said she was sure Dave Watson had made trails
all over the Horseshoe Range so if they only
struck one of his they would be certain it led
safely out somewhere, and for once Don agreed
with her.   So they rode along letting the ponies
pick their way up the first slopes of the mountain
where Sandy had told them the door was located.
There were no trees and very little underbrush,
only a stately stalk of Our Lady's Candle in
blossom here and there, or a great sprawling
growth of Spanish bayonet to avoid.   Sage grew
in sparsely scattered clumps, and the earth and
grass were already dry and yellow after a long
drought following the early spring rains.

The higher they ascended the hotter it grew,
even with a light breeze freshening up through
the canyon.   Still it was better than following

the low trail that led along the dry creek bed. Instead of riding directly up, Don rode back and forth the way old trail riders used to, easing the ponies from steep climbing.

"You know," Tim said once, as they came along a particularly steep stretch and the ponies hugged the side of the cliff, "this looks kind of familiar to me, I mean the way you can see Lookout way off there, and that mesa with the fringe of eucalyptus on it, it's just like the place where we found Pablo and Pinto."

"That was on this side of Lookout itself. Gee, look at the road runner."

They halted to watch the big bird as it raced along ahead of the ponies and ducked into the underbrush with Powder after it in mad pursuit. Tim lifted her head and took in a deep breath of the wonderful mountain air. "I love to get way up like this until you can look down and see all the little hills and other mountains below you like a relief map at school, and still keep on going higher."

"Well, you're going higher all right," Don assured her, as he looked back. "We've just started up. I'm wondering if we could cut around that big point yonder and save going clear to the top. It must come out on the east side of the mountain and that would be right over Blind Canyon. Sandy said he thought the door was about two miles up, didn't he?"

"Yes, just about that far." Tim was still staring off at the mesa opposite them. "Don, I'm positive that's the same place, there are all those rocks, see, where Pablo hid from us."

"What if it is?" asked Don, "come along, that doesn't matter." He started off around the jutting shoulder and found the way easier riding for the ponies. Once they had made the half circle and come out on the east side, they found themselves directly above Blind Canyon, but so high that the bottom, where the creek ran, was hidden from sight by trees and the various twists and turnings the canyon made as it cut into the range.

"Oh, Don, do look at the color in those rocks," Tim called out. "They look as if they were all carved out in heads and faces." The canyon widened out into a magnificent view ahead of them, a great rose and ochre gorge of mighty rock masses that showed the drift in long diagonal lines of strata. "What's the matter?" Don had dismounted and was examining the ground.

"Looks as if there'd been a trail here once, but it hasn't been travelled in a long while. You wait here with the ponies till I see how far it goes."

"Powder, you stay here," Tim called as Don disappeared down the bend of the trail, but Powder trotted on just the same as if it were also necessary for him to find out what was beyond. Tim waited until the two ponies grew restive and stepped back away from the brim of the steep canyon rim. Each time she whistled, Tim heard Don's answer though it sounded farther and farther away, so she knew he was safe, and when he finally did come plodding back he was hot and red faced, but satisfied. They could ride the ponies on for about half a mile, he told her, and there was a good place to leave them while they went on the rest of the way on foot.

"But why can't they get down too? Isn't there a trail?"

"No, not when you get beyond a big rock that's hanging right over the edge of the trail. It seems to stop there, but the ground is rough and rocky, and it's easy to get a foothold. Only don't miss your step because if you do, you'll just be out of luck, that's all, and you'll find yourself dangling over the brink on the end of a rope."

Don was taking off the coil of rope from his saddle horn. " I'm going to lead Dusty because he's limping, anyhow, on the off leg from stepping in a gopher hole back yonder."

" I can climb better than you, Don, so if anyone needs the rope it will be you," Tim started to argue, but Don went on ahead along the narrow winding trail, and all she could do was follow his lead or be left behind.

After they had travelled for some time Don called back to her to wait a minute. He left Dusty standing alone and went forward like a skulking Indian keeping close against the rock wall. It was not very pleasant waiting for him on the narrow trail, with hundreds of feet below her a sheer drop to the bottom of the canyon. And Chapo was swishing his tail about and moving restlessly every time Dusty moved back a little.

" What is it? " she called.

" Come on," Don shouted back, and all at once he appeared unexpectedly close. It was as if his head bobbed up at her over the rocks. " The trail ends just ahead of us, and we'll have to walk both ponies because the ground's crumbled away in one place. Landslide, I guess, but they can make it if we let them alone. You can see where a whole slice of the mountain has just caved-in, but there's a good place for the ponies to wait while we go on."

Tim swung down from her saddle dubiously. Whenever it was a choice between Chapo or herself on a narrow trail she always let Chapo do the leading, but she did as Don had said now, and both ponies behaved splendidly; as if they knew all about it. Once they managed to get around the big rock, it was not so hard to scramble down to the broad ledge that projected from the side of the gorge like a shelf. Here was where they would leave the ponies, Don said, but when Tim wanted to hitch them to something, even a bush, he told her she didn't *savez* horses, as Pablo said. They would no more stray off over the edge and fall than wild goats might. The worst they might do was to go on back the

way they had come and even if they did, it would
be easy to find them again.

"Suppose they take a notion and go all the
way to the ranch without us?" Tim asked.

"They won't, they know enough to stand
around until we get back. I've got the rope and
we won't need anything else because we're coming straight back."

"That's all right, but my supplies go right
along on my back. Sandy says never to part
from your grub when you're in the wilderness." Tim unstrapped her lunch and blanket
and loaded up resolutely. "Here, you might
carry the hatchet anyway."

Don led the way, picking footholds cautiously
on the rocky, crumbling ground. He grumbled
but waited for her to catch up with him and took
the coiled rope around one shoulder and the
hatchet and his own lunch box. On second
thought he roped the last two together, and left
his hands free.

"Oh, look," Tim called suddenly, "there's the
black pine, Don, and we're past it already."

They paused to look down the gorge and there
was the black sprawling outline of pine against

the rose-colored rock, but they were at least a quarter of a mile from it. There was no sign of any recent trail, however, as they had hoped to find beyond the big rock, but Tim said perhaps there had been one before the landslide, and it had been broken off like a crust.

"Then it must begin again on the other side where the landslide stopped," Don said. "Let's find out."

Powder was far ahead of them and barking frantically. Tim wanted to find out what he had cornered, so while Don started to climb up to the higher ledges where the trail should have been continued from the big rock, she stood whistling to Powder, but he only barked louder, and finally rushed toward her. Along his back a ridge of hair stood up in the funniest way possible, and his eyes were excited as he pranced before her, backing and barking as if he were trying to warn her not to go any further.

"I suppose you've chased some poor little rabbit down his front door," Tim said, but Powder dove completely out of sight and after a moment she saw he was making a detour down the steep cliff as if he were trying to get around something ahead of her. She hesitated, wondering whether to wait or follow Don, and then she heard a sound that could never be mistaken once it was heard, the warning rattle of a snake.

Tim was too startled to call out for help, and Don was far ahead of her now, climbing higher. The rattlesnake lay just ahead of her, coiled ring on ring like a lariat on the bare hot earth beside a pile of crushed rock. She could see its eyes glitter like water in sunlight as it watched her, and a queer numb dizziness seized her. Her mouth was dry and stiff, and her feet seemed buried deep in the ground. It was only a few seconds, but to Tim it seemed hours. Then racing up behind the snake came Powder and he leaped for it from the rear. The long body thrashed about like a whirling whiplash around and around the terrier's sturdy strong little frame, but Powder's teeth were buried in its neck and when it was over a perfectly good dead rattler lay limply on the ground and Powder wagged his stubby tail and sneezed and tried to paw at his nose and cock one delighted ear at the same time.

"Darling," exclaimed Timmie, "you've saved

my life. Oh, Don, Don, where are you anyway?"

"What's the matter?" shouted back Don, out of sight some place.

"Powder's killed a big rattler, and the place is just full of them." She was so excited she could hardly stir, but Powder started barking again and making wild prances before the pile of rock, and all about it there seemed to be sluggishly stirring slate-brown bodies in the hot sunlight, as the dog disturbed their mid-afternoon siesta.

She started then to get away, climbing up the steep slope as fast as she could, and Don's answering shout told her he was returning to help her, but just as she grasped hold of a jutting ledge of rock, it crumbled under her weight, and she found herself clinging to a clump of cactus that stung and pricked her hands like thousands of needle points.

"Oh, Don, I can't hold on any longer," she cried.

CHAPTER XX

" You wait for me, don't you dare let go,"
Don shouted back, and he came down the steep
grade like a wild goat, the rope coiled in his
hands.

" But I can't, throw me the rope." Tim did
not feel terribly frightened, she was only thinking how her hands hurt and how far it would be
going down once she did let go. She dug her
toes into the ground to try and make a foothold
for herself, and relieve the strain on her hands,
but the more she dug at it the more the earth
just crumbled away under her feet. Suddenly
she felt something slip down around her in coils
and it startled her, even though she was expecting Don to throw the rope—it was so much like
a snake. It tightened around her waist with a
jerk.

" It's all safe," Don called. " I've got it
around a boulder."

" You would," Tim said; " supposing it comes
rolling down on me." She held on to the rope

and slowly steadied herself until she could climb up with Don's helping hand. Once beside him she sat down limply. "Whew, that was certainly dreadful. Did you see that whole ledge of rock just start and break away when I tried to hang on? And the rattlers, you should just see them, Don. Look down there where Powder's barking." She tried to point out the snakes to him, but Don was not even looking their way. He was staring at the open gash in the ground where the rock ledge had given way.

"Gee, Tim, look there," he exclaimed, "that looks like free gold!"

Tim glanced to where he was pointing, and saw the bright sparkle of something in the dry earth under the dislodged ledge. "It may be just mica or quartz," she said, "don't be foolish. You wouldn't find it like that."

"Yes, you would too. This was all a river bed in this canyon, and the water's washed away the earth for years and left the gold behind, don't you see? Sandy says a canyon's the best place to hunt for gold." He dug with both hands into the hole like Powder after a gopher, and Tim watched with growing excitement. "See it,"

Don cried, " there's some more, and look at this."
He lifted out a nugget, smaller than the one
Sandy had shown them, but still a real gold
nugget.

Powder's barking became louder and nearer,
and he came toward them, scrambling excitedly
and half falling. He had evidently found out
that too many rattlers are not a good experiment
for any dog no matter how good a sport he might
be, and both Tim and Don made a dash for safety
also.

" If we go higher up, there aren't any snakes
there," Don said, and Tim followed him. They
did not realize that they were heading in the
opposite direction from where they had left the
ponies until they were well around the next curve
of the canyon wall, where they paused to rest.
Tim said they must get Pablo and let him in on
the secret; he wasn't a bit afraid of snakes because he knew the Indian way of charming them.
All at once she noticed Don had halted and was
staring, puzzled, at the way they had come, and
then down the canyon behind them.

" Didn't we leave the ponies back there on that
big ledge? " he asked.

Tim turned around and from where she and Don stood they could see the ledge. There was no sign of the ponies, however, not even along the upper trail.

"Oh, they've just wandered back by themselves," she said. "We'll find them waiting for us when we get back. I told you to hitch them to something."

"Well, if I had they might have gone tumbling over into the canyon. The ground around here isn't safe at all. It's all loose and cracked from rains, and I think we'd better keep on going this way until we find a place that looks good enough to climb over, instead of trying to go back that other way."

Tim agreed, mostly because she didn't want any possibility of landing again where there were snakes, and this way seemed much safer as they climbed higher. It was very warm, though, and she felt sorry she had brought along the blanket, but Don called to her that if she didn't stop saying how hot it was, he would chuck the hatchet back to her to carry too, since she wanted him to bring it along.

"You can have the rope too if you want to

since it came in so handy lassoing you," he added cheerfully.

"Don't be cross and fussy, we've been climbing for hours, and it does seem as if we ought to come out somewhere pretty soon. We're too far up Blind Canyon now to find the door, I know that, because it's way back near the pine. I don't see where you think you're going."

"Well, if you can't go back you have to go ahead, don't you?" Don demanded. He grinned at her. "I don't know where we're going, but if we keep on, we're going to find out."

"Do you mean that we're lost, Don?" Tim looked at him incredulously.

"Not just exactly lost, because all we have to do is cut straight west over the mountain and we must come out on the other side. And anyhow, if I really thought we were lost, all I'd have to do would be to light a fire as soon as it gets dark and Dave Watson would come over to find out what it was all about."

Tim heaved a sigh of relief. "I'm so glad you've got it all figured out, darling, because as you may have noticed, the sun is going down, and there's something besides rattlers up in these mountains that I don't like when we haven't a gun along."

"Not a thing around here but coyotes, and it isn't late, only around three. It just begins to look dark because we're in the canyon."

"Well, let's stop and rest a minute, I'm hungry too." Tim prepared to open up her lunch and get out a cold tamale, but Don stood looking about with half closed, troubled eyes. "I don't think we'd better stop, we ought to keep right on while we can."

"Do you think we may have to camp out tonight?" Tim asked. "I don't mind so long as we find a decent place where we're sure we can't roll off the edge."

"It looks wider up there," Don pointed just beyond them. "See there that bush grows out beside the rock. We might get up there where it looks as if it was better going and more level."

"Oh, but just look back at the canyon in this lovely light, rose and purple and gold. It seems as if the rocks are changing color."

"Never mind the rocks, hurry up, we can't waste any time over scenery, Tim, you ought to

know that. Gee, I don't want to stay out all
night and have to look after you. I didn't want
to tell you, but Tom said he heard mountain
lions are around up here. Slim killed one last
Saturday."

"I'll bet a cookie it was Slim that told about
it, and Joe or Sam that listened," laughed Tim.
"There aren't any mountain lions around here
in these little mountains, just coyotes and maybe
wildcats." Tim stopped and stood looking at
the face of the canyon above them. Of course,
she thought, it could be true, she just thought it
was a door she saw there, a large heavy timbered
door set deeply into the side of the mountain so
that it looked like the entrance to a tunnel in
the sloping ground. "Don," she said in a hushed
tone, "look, do you see it too?"

"Snakes?" Don didn't even look where she
pointed. "Here, Powder, come boy, sic 'em."

"It isn't snakes, goose, it's the door, look,
right up there behind those bushes, Don."

Don never said another word about snakes,
but came down half sliding in his haste to get
to her. Then he looked up and stared too, and
whistled. "Sure enough," he said, "there it is

all right. I'd like to see old Sandy's face this minute if he knew. How do you suppose anybody ever got a real door up there?"

"Maybe they put it there from the inside of the mountain, there must be a tunnel or something." Don gave Tim a long look of reluctant admiration.

"Well, you found it," he said, "and you've got the right idea about that door too. It's some sort of a hiding place, or maybe outlaws used it for a secret treasure cave."

"But how far can you go in the mountain, I wonder," Tim said eagerly. "If they did set the door up from inside, the tunnel might lead into a cave. It wouldn't hurt just to see, would it, I mean, if we only pushed the door a little and looked inside."

"If it isn't barred or locked or something from inside. Remember what Sandy said about the skeleton."

"But wouldn't it be thrilling to push it open and find a real skeleton sitting there behind it?" Tim's eyes were wide and excited. "Oh, please, Don, come on, I'm not a bit afraid to try it. After we've come all this long way and there it is right in front of us, you wouldn't go back without trying to open it, would you? "

Tim pleaded while Don stared up at the door, and scratched his head. Certainly, as she said, there it was, right in front of them, the door they had longed to find and had hunted and hunted for, and now at the last minute, perhaps some inborn old Scotch sense of caution and safety first held Don back from venturing in. Tim begged so hard, however, just to climb up and give it a little push so she could peek in, only to see if it was open and if the skeleton was there, that was all, that at last Don gave way, and they started to climb up to the door.

The ground directly under it was too steep, but by skirting around on one side, they discovered what might have been some time footholds cut deeply into the earth, and braced with rock. These crumbled as they stepped on them, but held long enough to get them up to the door and Powder somehow managed to climb up after them. He was even more excited than the children, standing panting away, with his little red tongue lolling out as he eyed the door.

" It opens right into the mountain," Tim exclaimed, when she saw the rusty old hinges. "Like a gnome's cave, or the trolls, oh, Don, remember 'In the hall of the mountain king'? It's like that."

She began to hum it, the queer, slow movement, as it was played at school sometimes, as if a whole long line of trolls were trying to file down into some mountain kingdom. "I think it's barred, though, on the inside, don't you?"

Don put his shoulder against the door and pushed gently at first, then harder, but the door held fast.

"Oh, let's both try." Tim caught up the hatchet where Don had dropped it with the rope. "Couldn't we wedge it open with this, Don?" She took it and pounded as hard as she could on the door until the echo of the blows sounded far down the canyon.

"You can't do it that way," Don lost his caution now. "Give it to me, you only make it stick harder that way." He took the hatchet and used it as a lever to force the door loose. There was no sign of any lock, so they were sure now that it must be barred inside, but all at once it gave way without warning, and fell in with such unexpected force that both of them fell with it, and staggered over into the space beyond.

" Well, anyway, we got it open," Tim laughed, as she brushed the dust and sand from her face and hair. " It's just a cave, Don, and there isn't any skeleton at all."

" It isn't a cave, it's a tunnel," said Don, when he stood up, and examined the inner frame of the doorway. Overhead were heavy timbers shoring up the roof of the tunnel just as he had seen them in old mining cut-ins around Frisbee, the long shafts dropped perpendicularly from the top and the tunnels made on different levels with openings out of the side of the mountain into the canyon. " It's just the entrance to some old level," he said.

" Just? " repeated Tim. " Goodness, what more do you want? It may be Sandy's old lost Spirit mine, Don, for all we know. Oh, why didn't we bring along the flashlight, the one thing we needed? "

" The one thing I brought along, you mean," Don drew the flashlight out of his pocket, but it turned out to be his own, not the long round one from the car. But at least it gave a light, and the two stepped eagerly into the low passage-way.

"It smells awfully," said Tim, "stuffy and earthy, doesn't it? Go on, Powder, you stay outside and wait for us, you'll think you've got to hunt gophers in here, and get your nose all sandy."

Powder obeyed reluctantly, and stood just outside the door looking eagerly and anxiously after them. "It must have been a gold mine," Don said. "Look here, here's an old pick." It stood leaning against one side of the passage as if it had only been left there the day before, only that the iron head was rusted. Don picked it up in both hands and looked at the handle, with the flashlight. "See," he said, "it's got initials cut in the handle, J. W."

"If we only knew the name of the skeleton," Tim exclaimed. "Let's go farther in. It seems to dip down over there."

"You look out where you go, it may just drop you off into an old shaft or something," warned Don, and he followed her doubtfully as she walked on, eager to see what lay ahead. Then without any warning there came a strange sound almost like an earthquake, a dull rumbling and tremor about them as if the whole mountain were seized with a chill, and the earth fell in a land-slide carrying down with it the timbered door and shutting out all daylight. Almost as quickly as it came there was utter silence and the two children faced each other in the tunnel. Tim was the first to recover her senses.

"It's only some earth falling in front of the doorway," she said cheerfully, "turn on the light, Don. We can dig our way right out with the pickaxe."

Don pressed the button and the flashlight showed only too plainly what had happened. The whole tunnel was solidly choked around the exit with rock and earth to the top, and part of the old timbers that had been used as shoring, had crashed in. Tim held the light while Don started to cut a way out with the pickaxe, but at every blow new quantities of earth tumbled from overhead, and he stopped.

"It'll all drop in on us if I do that," he said. "Gee, that happened awfully quick. I hope it didn't get Powder."

"He'd have yelped if it had," Tim said sensibly. "We'll have to dig ourselves out, Don, if we do it with our hands. We can't stay in here. Let's try doing it very carefully. Just burrow out like a rabbit." She lay flat down on the ground to show him what she meant, and started to scoop away the earth at the very bottom, just a little at a time as if she were making a tunnel in the sand. "Here," she called, "give me the pickaxe, and I'll stick the handle through until we get to air."

"Look out now, or you'll have the whole mountain down on our necks," warned Don, but she took the pickaxe and pushed the handle ahead of her first into the scooped-out place she had made with her hands. It seemed to go in easier the harder she pushed it, but when she got to the head, there was no breaking through into the air; it only stuck fast. "Oh, dear," Tim said, "I'll try it in another place," and she gave the pickaxe a pull to get it out, when another slide came, and she was covered with dirt and crumbled rock. Don caught hold of her and dragged her back, coughing and sneezing, as she shook the sand out of her hair.

"Perhaps you'll stop now," he scolded. "Do

you want to get all squashed and leave me in here alone with your dead body?"

"All right, but we'll have to try and get out the other way then," Tim protested. "We can't just sit here and wait for people to find us because they won't know where we are."

"Yes, they will," Don answered. "I didn't take any chances coming on this trip. I wrote a letter to Sandy and I mailed it yesterday at the post office, and he comes after his mail Saturdays. I told him where we were going, and if we didn't come back, he was to come and get us."

Tim groaned. "Aren't you wonderful? Don't you know that Sandy's changed his day to go to Sam's? He goes Wednesdays now instead of Saturdays."

"How do you know?" demanded Don.

"He told me so, himself, the last time I saw him, when he came up to look at the mail plane."

CHAPTER XXI

IT seemed too dreadful even to realize, at first, that they could be imprisoned underground in the mountain, fifteen miles from home, with Powder the only living creature that really knew where they were.

"But the landslide may have buried him alive too," said Tim. "He would surely have gone back to Sandy anyway, and made him understand there was something wrong."

"The ponies will go home, but you can't tell when because they'll wait around for us to come back to them." Don had his flashlight and walked back and forth slowly in the tunnel trying to see how far it extended ahead of them. "This is a cross-cut to an old mine all right, and it looks as if that landslide had opened up a big ore vein, see there?" He threw the light on the crumbled earth and rock where it had caved in, and Tim drew in a deep breath as she caught the sparkle of gold.

"Oh, Don, it *is* there, isn't it, after all they've

said. Sandy and his Indian were right, but maybe we'll be wishing we could swap it for a good sandwich, just as he said. It's awfully musty and earthy down here. I'm glad we had a chance to let in a little fresh air when we opened the door. It will last us quite a while. Do you suppose we could live in here until Wednesday?"

"Sure," Don said cheerfully, "we'd last much longer than that. Why, miners have lived for weeks when they had food and water. We'll have to put ourselves on rations, just a bite now and then and a sip of the water. It's a good thing we brought the lunch along."

"Yes, and I'm glad that Powder isn't with us, for you never can tell what might happen if we were really starving. You're apt to eat anything."

"Now listen, we're in here, and we've got to keep up our courage and stick by each other, but if you start talking about eating Powder ——"

"I didn't say we were going to eat him, we can't anyway because he isn't in here. I only said ——"

"Well, don't say it. I've got to keep my

head and think this out.   It can't be so very far through this cross-cut to the main shaft."

"Maybe that's caved in too."   Tim kept closely at his heels as he went slowly and cautiously ahead of her, holding the flashlight so that it threw a circle of light before them into the dark recesses of the tunnel.   " I feel exactly like Clementine, don't you remember? " and she sang dolefully:

> " In a cavern, by a canyon,
>   Excavating for a mine,
>   There lived a miner, forty-niner,
>   And his daughter Clementine."

Her voice seemed to echo far in the distance and Don halted and listened to it.   " That sounds as if it went a long way back.   Maybe there's a cave beyond there.   Keep close behind me, Tim, because sometimes there's a quick drop to a lower level."

" Just think, here we are in our gold mine at last, and it is ours because we've discovered it, and there may be millions in gold all around us, and they'll find our poor little skeletons in here some day.   It just goes to prove that gold isn't worth a thing when you need help.   If we come

to a fork in this tunnel, how will you know which
way to take, Don? ”

“ We'll try both,” said Don. “ Wait a minute, we ought to take specimens with us, in case
we do get out, so they'll believe us.” He stopped
and moved the light about on the dislodged rock
and earth. Tim helped to break off some of the
pieces that sparkled most. It was like being shut
up in Aladdin's cave, she thought; you just
helped yourself to gold and silver. They walked
on for what seemed to be a very long distance
and still the tunnel stretched on ahead of them,
but they noticed that the air grew better as if
there were a current coming in from some place
beyond them. All at once Tim felt her feet
getting damp and stooped down to touch the
earth. “ Don, it's all damp here,” she said,
“ don't you feel it? ”

Don stopped and turned the flash down. Certainly there seemed to be a seepage under their
feet. The ground was like an old sponge, soft
and soggy. “ Maybe we're coming to an underground river like Sandy told us about,” Tim said
excitedly.

“ You can go on supposing anything in a place

like this," Don told her. " I don't think it's anything but a trickle of water somewhere near here; underground spring, probably. Maybe we'll have to come back to it and it will keep us from dying of thirst."

They started off again, and walked in silence for another long distance through the strange, narrow tunnel. It was shored up with old timber, but every now and then they came to a place where a plank had fallen down, and it seemed as if it might all cave in on their heads at any moment. Then Don noticed that they seemed to be going uphill to another level, and he told Tim to wait for him while he went ahead to find out what they might be coming to.

" I won't let you go away from me," she said obstinately. " Do you suppose it is night time yet, Don? I'm getting sleepy. I wonder if the ponies or Powder have had time to get back to the ranch so that people will be coming after us? "

" If he goes anywhere, Powder will just cut across the desert to Sandy's, and he'll be sound asleep. I think the ponies will stick around until morning waiting for us, before they start back to the ranch. We're all right, Tim, we're coming out on the main shaft of this thing, and it must let out somewhere."

"But I'm awfully tired. I don't want to go another step." Tim stopped and leaned against the side of the tunnel and immediately there was a shower of small stones and dirt. "Oh, dear me, I feel as if this old mountain were going to tumble down around us like a pack of cards," she exclaimed. "You can't even touch it without its crumbling."

Don did not reply. He had stopped, too, and stood facing the tunnel, holding the flash directly in front of him, peering at something ahead. In the ring of light thrown by the flash lay a strange object, directly at the end of the tunnel. It might have been the side of an elephant turned towards them, if such a thing could have been down there. Don looked, and blinked his eyes, then stared at it again to see if it moved.

"What is it?" asked Tim sleepily. "What's the matter now?"

"Look there," whispered Don. "It may be only a big rock, but it sure looks mighty funny to me."

Tim's hands caught his arm. "Oh, Don, I

think—I'm sure it's a body." She spoke in a hollow, frightened tone. " One of those prehistoric things the professor was hunting for. It does look dead, doesn't it, because if it were alive, the light would bother it."

" It's awfully queer." Don frowned and switched the light about on it, up and around and under it, but it looked about the same—a mysterious grayish brown object, rounded like a body, and almost half filling the tunnel. Still there was no fur on it, and no sign of any legs or a head.

" Oh, the dickens," said Don impatiently. " I'm going to see what it is. It isn't alive anyway ——"

" Oh, but Don, wait a minute; look, it's got a tail, a long one, curled around it, don't you see? " Tim whispered tragically as she pointed to something that lay coiled about the strange object.

But Don kept walking toward it. " It's not a tail," he said flatly. " It's a rope."

When they finally reached the mysterious object, it turned out to be an old mine bucket, shaped like a big barrel, tilted over on its side, with a heap of old, rotting rope and some rusty

chains lying beside it. Don gave it a kick just
to make up for the thrill of fear and the scare
it had given them, but as he did so, it rolled over,
and there lay what seemed to be a heap of old
rags, but when the flashlight was turned on them,
Tim gave a cry and hid her face against Don's
shoulder.

"Gee," he said softly, "it's a skeleton!"

"Oh, Don, can't we get out? I don't want to
look at it." Tim turned her face away when he
bent down to examine it. "It's just what Sandy
said, we might find the owner behind the door."

"Well, that's all right, he wouldn't mind now;
maybe he'd be glad if he knew someone had
found him." Don looked up. The tunnel ended
at the bottom of an old mine shaft, and fresh
air was coming to them from somewhere overhead. All he could see were four converging
walls and darkness. It was like looking at the
tunnel upside down. The shaft seemed to rise
up through the heart of the mountain, and there
was a ladder built straight against one side, of
rough cross-bars of wood nailed to uprights. He
took hold of it and shook it, but it did not promise
much safety. "We'll have to try and climb out

of here, I guess," he said. "I was afraid the shaft had caved in too. You just wait here for me with the flashlight and I'll climb up to the top and see where we are."

"And leave me down here alone with that?" said Tim, indignantly. "I'm going up too."

"But a girl can't climb a ladder like that, Tim. Why, it goes straight up in the air for several hundred feet, and it's shaky."

"I don't care what it's like," Tim said firmly. "You're not going to leave me down here with a skeleton for company. Supposing you fall too, and then here I'd be with you both. I know I can climb that ladder. All you do is keep on going and don't look down."

"Then wait till I tie a rope around you, and let me go first," Don ordered, but it was too late. Tim was climbing up the wooden ladder and all he could do was to follow. He stuck the flashlight in his back pocket, with the catch fixed, so that it threw the light above them, which helped a lot. It was bad enough to climb the rickety, unsafe ladder, but it would have been much worse if they had had to do it in utter darkness.

"I'm going to rest a minute," Tim warned, and stopped, one arm hooked into the ladder's cross piece. She glanced up at the top of the shaft, now about half-way from them. "I don't see any sky up there, Don."

"Shafts aren't open at the top, they just come out on a tunnel too, cross-cut in from the side of the mountain. Say, don't shake the ladder so when you climb, just remember I'm down below."

"I suppose he started down in that bucket and the rope broke," Tim said thoughtfully, looking down at the bottom of the shaft. "Do you suppose Sandy or Dave Watson will know who he was?"

"I don't want to think about him until I get out of this," retorted Don. "Just you keep right on going up, will you, and stop talking about the last one that fell down."

"All right," sighed Tim as she started to climb again, "only we'll probably feel very grateful to him when we find we're the owners of his gold mine."

When they finally reached the last round of the ladder, they found themselves in a sort of old shed built against the shelving mountain side, that led into a dugout where the opening of the mine shaft was. "He must have lived right here," Tim said wonderingly, as they looked around at the old makeshift bed with a couple of blankets on it, and the table with cupboard nailed up above it and a few dishes neatly placed there. "Look, Don, isn't that queer, doesn't it make you almost shiver?" She pointed to a sign painted in black letters and nailed up over the door.

SPIRIT MINE.

"We'll change the name of that right away," Don said. "Let's get out in the fresh air. I'm dizzy from that climb."

They opened the door and found the entrance so overgrown with underbrush and tangled vines that it was completely hidden from sight, and it was hard to work their own way out. But once they found themselves standing on the rocky, wind-swept mountain, Tim pointed to a familiar outline in the moonlight. "There's Lookout, Don. Oh, isn't it good to be outside?"

She stretched her arms wide, her face lifted to

the sky, as she breathed in deeply, but Don was already gathering handfuls of dry grass and sagebrush to start a fire with on a big rock. Tim helped too, tying the grass into knotted bunches the way Estrella had taught her to do to make it burn longer. Don had matches, and once the fire was lighted, the flame rose in the air like an Indian signal flare.

"Dave will be sure to see it, and probably they've missed us by now and got out search parties, so this will show them where we are," Don said. "Now let's eat. Gee, isn't it good we don't have to go on rations? I could eat all we've got right now."

He spread the blanket out on the ground, and stretched out on it wearily while Tim opened up the lunches and sat cross-legged near him. Now that the danger was all over, they felt famished, and devoured all that was left of the lunch and drank all the water that was in the canteen. They would take turns sleeping and keeping watch, Don said, but in the end both of them fell sound asleep, rolled in the blanket, while the lone fire burned a little while, flickered and went out.

CHAPTER XXII

It was bright daylight when they awakened from the long sleep of exhaustion. Tim sat up and blinked her eyes, not believing all that she saw before her—the morning beauty of the mountains and old Lookout looming up to their right, and below the great golden stretch of the desert.

"Don," she called, "it's morning and the fire is out."

Don woke with a start and shook himself as he jumped up. "We sure slept, didn't we? It doesn't matter anyway, because now we can find our way back all right. I know exactly which way to go to hit that trail we came up on from the canyon. All we have to do is strike out from here straight down that way, and it isn't hard going either."

"There isn't a single bite of anything left for breakfast." Tim hunted around vainly for even a crust, but there was nothing left of their lunch. Not that it mattered, Don said, because they'd be home at the ranch by noon and get plenty to eat. Tim didn't just see how they were going to walk all the way across the desert by noon, and up through Las Flores Canyon, but she didn't say anything to discourage him. Rolling up the blanket, they started off to tramp back, Don doing the scouting.

Then Tim remembered something. They must put up a stake to their mine, she said, people always staked out a mine when they found it. Don said no, that was only for a mining claim, but Tim wanted to be on the safe side, so she took a scrap of paper from the piece the lunch was wrapped up in, and wrote on with Don's stub of a pencil:

> " Staked by the McLeans,
> June 17th, 1928."

Don took some pieces of wood out of the hut and drove them deep into the ground with the hatchet, and stuck the paper on one of them. Then they shut the door of the hut and nailed it up, and put another piece of paper on the side with the same thing written on it. " Not that anyone will come here, but because it's the custom," Tim said gravely.

It was still cool on the mountain in the early morning and they started off at a good pace, taking a direct route toward the desert to the south. The long sleep had refreshed both of them, and they were eager to get back home and spring their surprise.

"It is mighty queer, though, that nobody seems to have missed us," Don said. "Even if the ponies didn't come back to the ranch, you'd think Father and Tom would have started out after us when we didn't show up last night."

"Perhaps they didn't miss us until this morning, you know how they are," Tim answered. "Father would say we could take care of ourselves anywhere, and go to bed without worrying. Of course, if Mother were home, she'd have everyone out hunting us from the sheriff to Pablo. I can just see Estrella scolding around when we never showed up for dinner, and this morning when they discover that we're still missing, she'll have seventeen fits all at once."

They kept on walking until Tim said she had never realized a mountain could have so much room on it, but Don told her as long as they knew they were travelling south toward the desert, they couldn't help but reach it. And besides, they might meet Dave Watson coming to look for them; naturally he would hunt all through the mountains as soon as Mr. McLean gave the alarm. But after what seemed to be hours, when the sun was well up in the sky, Don stood still and looked about him puzzled. Somehow the desert appeared to have moved away from them, and the land about was barren and chaotic, with great masses of strange rock formation, and hardly a cactus in sight.

" That looks just like the rim of the canyon where we climbed over going down," Tim called his attention to the distant edge of ground outlined against the skyline. It did look rather familiar, Don agreed, and they made for it as fast as they could in the heat. And then sounds came to them, shouts and voices from somewhere far down in the canyon. Tim ran excitedly forward to look over the rocks, and lay flat down to edge herself along to the very brink.

" Don McLean," she exclaimed, after one good look. " Do you see that? They're looking for us."

Don leaned far over to see what was going on

below, and his eyes almost popped out. It did
look as if most of the population of Frisbee had
come down into Blind Canyon. They were
strung out along the trail where the children had
travelled, and sprinkled on the sides of the canyon, but most of them were gathered around one
spot, about a mile past the big rock where the
trail broke off.

And here it seemed as if they were all shovel-
ling away at the side of the mountain where the
landslide had been, like so many ants. "Tim,"
Don said in a voice of awe, "gee, do you know
what they think they're doing? They're digging
us out."

"Maybe they think we're dead." Tim put her
hands to her mouth and gave a long call,
"Yee-ooo!" like the cowboys used. Her clear
healthy young voice rang out through the canyon, and they could see at once it was heard.
From far below there came a faint answering
shout, and the tiny black figures along the cliff
seemed to hurry together. Tim wondered what
she could wave down to them, when Don solved
the problem by whipping off his shirt and using
it for a signal flag. When they saw a flash of

white waving in answer, they knew that they had been seen.

" Oh, Don, they're coming back after us," Tim cried happily. " Wasn't that marvelous though, to be way up here and see them digging us out of the side of the mountain? I'll bet a cookie everyone's down there; Sandy, and Sam and Pablo and Mr. Watson, and here we are, on top."

" Well, don't stand talking about it for pity's sake," Don said, " I'm starving." And he started off as fast as he could walk toward the rescue party. The first person to meet them was Pablo, running like a young deer ahead of the rest. All of his stolidity had vanished. He laughed and danced when he saw them and grabbed at their hands to shake them eagerly.

" Me find," he exclaimed. " Me come after you. Me go up Blind Canyon, me find dog."

" Oh, then Powder is alive," cried Tim. " Isn't that good? Where did you find him, Pablo? Didn't the ponies go back home? "

" Ponies wait for you come back," Pablo declared. " They no go way back home, they stand and wait for you."

" Well, the old precious things, and we thought of course they'd trail along back to the ranch —— Oh, there's Father." And Tim flew to meet Mr. McLean, made one jump and landed close in his arms, with Don a close second.

" You certainly have stirred things up," he told them. " Here's Sandy and Dave and plenty more to help. Pablo went to look for you when you failed to show up for dinner ——"

" The mama say much-a go," Pablo put in soberly, his arms folded on his breast as he stood erect beside Tim.

" Then he came back with Powder and told about the landslide in the canyon, and the dog barking outside. We've been over here pretty nearly all night."

" Oh, you dear, I'm so sorry to have worried you, but listen," Tim drew away to look him full in the face, " we've found the old Spirit mine, and there's gold in it. Where are your specimens, Don? And there was a skeleton there at the bottom of the shaft; what do you think of that, Father?"

" It all sounds great and marvelous, but your mother and grandmother are getting into Oro on

the three-twenty to-morrow, and you've got to
hustle back home and get rested up." Mr.
McLean smiled as Sandy came hurrying up with
his curious long shambling stride.

" Did you find it? " he shouted when he was
still a long way off, and both the children called
back:

" Yes! "

" Skeleton and all," Tim added when he had
caught up with them. Dave came riding up.

" Oh, Mr. Watson, we did light a signal fire on
a rock for you to find us by, but we were so
sleepy we couldn't keep it up."

" You did, eh! Just let me catch you starting
any fires on the Horseshoe, and I'll turn you both
over to Slim to take to the sheriff," Dave's blue
eyes twinkled. " You two can start more trouble
than any other youngsters I know of; you get
the whole town all wrought up while you go
through a mountain like a couple of gophers."

" Gophers? " repeated Tim. " Do you know
what we've found? We've found the old lost
Spirit mine, and somebody's skeleton down there,
and we've staked it out and put our names on it."

" Not on the skeleton," Don corrected, " on

the mine, she means. Would it be ours, really, Mr. Watson, just because we found it again?"

"It's yours all right," said Dave. "That claim's been lying dead for around forty years to my knowledge, and the skeleton, say, Sandy, what was the name of that old fellow that was crazy and said the spirits told him where to find gold?"

"Never had a name," Sandy answered briefly. "Always called him Old Looney. That was long before my time, but I've known folks that could remember him. He just disappeared. I'd say that it was a good deal more than just luck that led you two youngsters to that door."

"Come along," called Mr. McLean, "the ponies are waiting for you down below."

"Don't you even want to see the hut or the entrance to the mine?" asked Tim. "It's only about three or four miles from here, isn't it, Don?"

"Not right now, daughter, it's home for all of us after a hard night's work," her father said. "Perhaps you don't know how we all felt thinking you two might be buried under that landslide."

Tim hardly heard him. She had heard a joyful bark in the distance, and rushed to meet Powder and clasp his delighted wriggling little body in her arms.

The next day when the express pulled into Oro, Tim and her father met it. The boys had stayed in school for exams, and Tom was away, so Tim had to represent the family. Mrs. Mc-Lean, after the first embrace, held her at arm's length, and presented her to Grandmother, and Tim was quite relieved to see that her new outfit made a good impression. Grandmother was slim and dark eyed, with curly gray hair, and a quick dimpling smile like her mother's, and Tim's heart warmed to her as she felt herself duly cuddled up on the drive home.

" Tim and I've been attending to a little special business to-day," Mr. McLean said, just as they were turning up into the canyon. " We dropped into the Recorder's office, and put on file her claim and Don's to the lost Spirit mine."

He turned and smiled confidentially.

" Oh, but it's all the family's," protested Tim eagerly. " And Sandy ought to have some of it too because he told us first about the door in the mountain, and Pablo ought to have some because he went after us when we were lost."

"There'll be enough for all when you get through," her father answered. "Chandler Thorpe told me this morning it was one of the places he had come out to try and find. If what he says is true, it's one of the richest lodes in this part of the state. The landslide evidently loosened it all up at that end, and exposed the vein."

Tim was silent for a minute, thinking very hard, then she said, "I wonder if we couldn't have Mr. Thorpe show us what to do with the mine. Now, Father, I don't mean that you couldn't, but he's got the money and backing and everything, and we haven't. I'd like to have Margot and Dick share in it too, if it would keep them out here with us."

"Suits me. He's the best they've got back East," Mr. McLean said, and Tim sighed with relief.

But that night when the celebration over the home-coming was over, and all the visitors had left, Tim went over to where Don lay sprawled out on the Indian rug before the big open fire and lay down beside him, very close. Don flung